POWYS SERVICE

SOLD

DATE

PRICE

The Bullfrog Trail

By the same author

The Ghost Riders
Brogan: Passing Through
Brogan's Mexican Stand-off
Luther's Quest
Brogan for Sheriff
Brogan: Fool's Gold
Brogan and the Bull
Zeke and the Bounty Hunter
Brogan: Shepherd's Gold
A Town Called Zero
Brogan Takes Toll
Thirteen Days
Brogan: To Earn a Dollar
Brogan and the Judge Killer
Brogan: Kidnapped
Caleb the Preacher
Brogan: Blood Money
Pioche Vendetta
The Hunter Hunted
Gringo
Maverick
Black Day in No-Name
Riverdale Showdown
Double Take

The Bullfrog Trail

L.D. TETLOW

A Black Horse Western

ROBERT HALE · LONDON

© L.D. Tetlow 1999
First published in Great Britain 1999

ISBN 0 7090 6348 2

Robert Hale Limited
Clerkenwell House
Clerkenwell Green
London EC1R 0HT

Photoset in North Wales by
Derek Doyle & Associates, Mold, Flintshire
Printed and bound in Great Britain by
WBC Book Manufacturers Limited, Bridgend

ONE

Brogan McNally, saddletramp, struggled out of his oilskin coat and threw it across his saddle, shook his hat vigorously in a useless attempt to dry it out and gazed through the grimy window of the saloon at the warm, inviting interior and eventually stomped through the door, his feet pounding the bare, wooden floor, again in a useless attempt to shake water from his jeans. Six men sitting round a table stared at him contemptuously for a moment but otherwise took no notice. Two other men leaning on the counter seemed not to look at him at all, but Brogan did not miss the fact that both men dropped their hands and gently eased the guns in their holsters. The very fact that they were wearing guns made Brogan wary; for the most part the average citizen did not wear a gun, there was normally no need to and, in fact, most seemed quite incapable of using handguns properly so the few who did were usually strangers or men employed to use them. These men did not give the impression of being strangers and that said to Brogan that they were employed to use them. He smiled to himself realizing that his gun also made him stand out, but his excuse was that he was a stranger who had just ridden into town.

'Whiskey!' he rasped, as he slouched on the counter. 'Make it a big one, I need it after ridin' through that lot.' Whiskey was not his normal drink, but at that moment he needed something to warm him up rather than quench his thirst.

He had just ridden for more than four hours through one of the worst rainstorms he had ever encountered – and he had encountered a great many in his time – and would normally have stopped to sit it out had there been any shelter, but flat, cattle plains rarely provided much cover and in this case none that he could see so he had been forced to keep on riding.

He had come across the town of Grover by pure chance, not having any idea where he was – something that was quite normal since neither time nor place had any real meaning in Brogan's life – and decided that since it appeared to be the only place he could shelter, he had little option, although he tended to avoid towns when he could. There had not even been the traditional barking dog to herald his arrival and apart from the men in the saloon there had been no sign of life at all which, considering the weather, he did not find surprising.

Eventually the two gunmen turned and stared at him. 'It must be the first time water's touched your skin in many a year,' sneered one of them. 'They say water brings out the smells an' in your case it's brought out a real stink.' All the men in the room laughed.

'They also say a dog allus smells its own shit first,' retorted Brogan. 'You must be gettin' confused.'

'We have us a funny feller!' sneered the man again, but this time accompanied his words by a stiffening of his body, obviously taken aback that some-one could have the nerve to talk to him in such a manner. 'You've got "saddlebum" written all over you. We don't like your type in Grover.'

'I'm surprised you can read anythin',' grunted Brogan, unable to resist the temptation to goad, then taking a mouthful of the rather rough whiskey and doing his best to hide the fact that he was choking. 'Don't worry, the feelin's mutual, I don't like places like Grover either.'

'Then drink up an' get on your way,' said the other man. 'We'd hate to keep you somewhere you didn't wanna be.'

'I'll leave when I'm good an' ready an' certainly not before this storm has passed,' said Brogan.

'I wasn't givin' you advice,' replied the man, 'I was givin' you an order.'

Very slowly and quite deliberately, Brogan looked round the room before replying, noting that the men at the table had all eased themselves away from it slightly in obvious preparation to move quickly should they need to. 'I take it you have some sort of authority?' he said eventually.

The man dropped his hand and tapped the handle of his gun, a sneer spreading across his lips. 'We've got all the authority we need right here,' he replied.

The two men glanced at each other, nodded and smiled and then took a step away from the counter as their hands dropped to their guns. They had barely gripped the handles when they suddenly found themselves staring in disbelief at the Colt now in Brogan's hand aimed steadily at them.

'Your move,' invited Brogan. 'What was that you

were sayin' about havin' the authority to run me out of town? I don't see no sheriff's badge on either of you.'

The onlookers had been so intent on watching the two that none of them could really say what had happened or just how fast on the draw the stranger had been, but the two men were almost convinced that the gun now in Brogan's hand had appeared by magic. They glanced at each other briefly and slowly drew their hands away from their guns very aware that they were up against someone who was possibly more capable than they were. For a few moments there were looks of hatred on their faces, expressions which Brogan had seen many times before and knew that he had just made enemies of two dangerous men. He knew from bitter experience that men like these would feel that they had in some way lost face and would be intent on restoring their standing.

'Real fancy!' sneered the one, casually leaning on the counter once again. 'I guess you was lucky an' caught us on the hop. I don't reckon you could do that in a straight face to face though.'

'Try me,' invited Brogan, slipping his Colt back into its holster. 'I don't reckon either of you would dare face any man who just might be faster'n you though. I'll even take you both at the same time.' He smiled ruefully to himself; he often made such challenges which, fortunately for him, were rarely taken up. Whilst he was fast on the draw and knew it, he also knew that one day he was going to come up against someone who was just that bit faster and not afraid to take him on. However, he had long since discovered that by challenging someone, they were normally not prepared to take the risk. This appeared to be the case this time.

'No saddlebum is worth the bother!' grunted the second man by way of saving some face.

Unbeknown to Brogan, Arnie Semple and Phil Grayson, the two men now facing him, had a reputation for being the fastest men in the territory and as far as anyone knew or could remember, they had never been outdrawn or outshot. Suddenly this dirty, wet, smelly saddletramp had ridden into town and had more or less destroyed that reputation in one draw. Not only that, he had issued a challenge which neither man had seemingly dared to take up. This fact had not been lost on the six men sitting at the table, but most of all it had not been lost on either Arnie Semple or Phil Grayson themselves who also knew that the incident would be common knowledge throughout the whole territory within a matter of hours and that there were many who would revel in their loss of face.

'I just came in for a drink an' to dry out a bit,' said Brogan, returning to his whiskey, which he drained and once again struggled to avoid coughing as the rough liquid coursed down his throat, and then ordered another. Brogan had his pride, too; to have succumbed to the effect of the whiskey would have been close to admitting that he was not normally a drinker of the amber fluid. 'I ain't lookin' for no trouble. I'll be on my way as soon as I can. In the meantime, can anyone tell me where the livery is? My horse deserves some decent food even if I don't.'

'Three buildin's down the street,' said one of the men at the table. 'I own the place. Charge is two dollars a night includin' feed.'

'A mite expensive,' said Brogan. 'Most only charge a dollar or even fifty cents in some places.'

'Then go find somewhere where they charge fifty cents,' grunted the man. 'Take it or leave it; it sure won't break my heart.'

'I'll take it,' nodded Brogan, realizing the futility of trying to haggle. 'But for that much I expect to be able to bunk down with my horse as well.'

'If the horse don't mind, I don't,' laughed the man, laughter taken up by everyone else except the two at the counter. Brogan smiled briefly, wishing that he had been paid one dollar every time the same thing had been said in the past, each believing that they were the frst to say it. 'That'll be two dollars – in advance.' He held out his hand. 'It ain't that I don't trust you, the fact is I don't. . . .' Further laughter from everyone. 'You could skip town before I get up in the mornin' or . . .' – he glanced at the two men at the counter – 'you could be dead in the mornin'.'

'I don't skip town owin' money to nobody,' said Brogan, digging into his pocket and producing two one-dollar coins which he handed to the man. 'As for bein' dead, you could be right, I could die in the night. Nobody knows when they is liable to just drop dead, but I don't think it'll be from a bullet, leastways not in this town.'

Arnie Semple and Phil Grayson could apparently take no more and stomped out of the saloon. Immediately there was a buzz of excited chatter amongst the six and the bartender. Eventually the chatter subsided and they all stared at Brogan.

'That sure was some fancy work,' said the owner of the livery, Frank Evans. 'I gotta warn you though, Mr . . . er. . . .'

'McNally,' replied Brogan. 'Brogan McNally. Just call me Brogan.'

'McNally ... er ... Brogan,' nodded the man. 'Frank Evans. I gotta warn you that what you just did has more or less signed your death warrant.'

'It ain't the first time,' grinned Brogan, 'an' unless I have been killed an' what you're lookin' at is a ghost, I'm still here.'

'Yeh, well, maybe,' continued Frank Evans. 'The point is them two is probably the fastest an' meanest men with guns this area has ever seen an' what you just did ain't gone down at all well with them, no sir. You can guarantee that they'll be out to get revenge or prove that what you just did was a lucky chance, that's all. By the way, was it just luck?'

'Maybe you'll never know,' grinned Brogan. 'Like you said, I could be dead in the mornin'. From what I could see through the rain, this looked like cattle country, I take it them two is what they usually call troubleshooters for one of the ranchers.'

'Troublemakers more like,' said one of the other men. 'Sure, you've got it, you seem to know what you're talkin' about. They work for Brad Stockwell, he owns all the land to the east of town.'

'And why should Brad Stockwell need men like that?' asked Brogan. He was not really interested – fully intending to leave as soon as he could – he was just curious or, more accurately, plain nosy.

'On account of him an' Heinrich Feldmann hate each other's guts an' each is tryin' to get his hands on some farms up in Bullfrog Pass,' replied Frank Evans.

'Wherever Bullfrog Pass is,' smiled Brogan, this time taking only a sip of his whiskey.

'Five miles due north,' said Frank Evans. 'It's a

long valley, settled by farmers long before either
Stockwell or Feldmann, or any of us come to that,
showed up.'

'And they don't want to move?' suggested Brogan.

'Strange lot,' said another of the six. 'They keep
themselves to themselves, only comin' into town to
sell their produce – which I gotta admit is pretty
damned good an' cheap – an' to buy whatever they
need, which don't seem to be that much since they
make most things themselves.'

'A very strict religious lot, too,' said Frank Evans.
'The world could be comin' to an end, but if it
happened on a Sunday they wouldn't do a damned
thing about it.'

'Each to his own,' smiled Brogan, satisfied that a
couple of simple questions had led to so much information. He now knew that two ranchers – Stockwell
and Feldmann – had a range war going and that each
was trying to get his hands on a valley named
Bullfrog Pass. He took another sip of his whiskey and
waited for someone to explain just why Bullfrog Pass
was so important. He did not have to wait long.

'The trouble is they settled in the wrong place,'
said another man. 'I know they was there first, but it
was still the wrong place, They should've known that
this is ideal cattle country an' that Bullfrog Pass is the
shortest way to drive cattle to the railroad.'

Now Brogan had it all.

'And Stockwell an' Feldmann each want to control
the valley?' he said. 'Maybe the farmers didn't know
about the railroad.'

'Guess not,' conceded the man. 'They was here
long before that was pushed through.'

'I guess I just made them two look small an''

Feldmann or his men will play it up,' smiled Brogan. 'That's their problem, but I'll be on the lookout for 'em. Now, after I've stabled my horse, where can I get somethin' to eat?'

'Only place is either here or the Black Diamond Saloon at the end of the street,' said the bartender – 'here' was named McGinty's Bar. 'This end of town is used by Stockwell's men an' the Black Diamond by Feldmann's.'

'An' where does that place you?' grinned Brogan.

'Somewhere in the middle,' replied the man, obviously a little uneasy. 'We minds our own business. It don't do for the likes of us to take sides.'

'The likes of you bein' the businessmen of the town,' guessed Brogan. The general nodding confirmed his guess. 'OK, so I eat here or this Black Diamond place. What do I get for my money?'

'I hate to turn business away,' said the bartender, 'but right now you spell trouble, trouble I can well do without. I suggest you try the Diamond, after what you just did you'll be more welcome there.' Brogan nodded; he could appreciate the bartender's problem and had to agree that under the circumstances he was probably right.

'OK, the Diamond it is,' he agreed. 'Do I just take my horse along to the livery an' help myself?'

'No problem,' replied Frank Evans, 'There'll be nobody else there but you. Hay an' feed is just inside the door an' there's water an' buckets outside.'

Brogan drained his glass, choked slightly, nodded at the six and went outside. He would not have been surprised to have seen Arnie Semple and Phil Grayson in the street but there was no sign of them, in fact there was no sign of anyone. He led his horse along the street and into the livery where he unsaddled her and brushed her down with a brush he found and then ladled out a good helping of oats and hay and placed a bucket of water alongside the oats.

There were two oil lamps burning which gave sufficient light to enable him to examine his surroundings and he quickly established just where everything was. He always liked to know where things were just in case he had to move suddenly during the night.

When he returned to the street, the rain appeared to have eased slightly and he located the Black Diamond at the far end of the street and walked slowly towards it, all the time taking in just what was where and looking and listening for signs of trouble.

The saloon was reached without any trouble and once again he peered through the grimy window to see who was inside. There appeared to be about ten men, four apparently playing cards, four leaning against the bar and two lounging with their feet up at a nearby table. Of the four at the bar, two seemed to be wearing guns, but as far as he could see all the others were unarmed. He pushed open the door and clattered towards the counter across the bare boards.

'They tell me I can get some food here,' he said to the bartender.

'An' who's "they"?' asked the bartender.

'The bartender at McGinty's,' replied Brogan.

The bartender looked up sharply. 'An' why should he do that?' he asked. 'He sells food too.'

'I guess I just made myself a mite unpopular there,' Brogan grinned.

'Unpopular?' queried the bartender.

At that moment another man came into the room, saw Brogan and hesitated slightly but then called the bartender over to him. Whispers passed between them along with frequent glances at Brogan. Eventually the bartender nodded and returned to Brogan.

'I guess you are unpopular there at that,' he agreed. In the meantime the man had attached himself to the four men at the counter and was in the process of repeating his story. 'Sure, I got food,' continued the bartender. 'I got beef steak an' I got beef stew.'

'A large steak sounds just fine to me,' said Brogan. 'How about some coffee?'

The bartender laughed. 'This is a bar, mister, I've got beer or I've got whiskey an' I've even got some gin an' some brandy, but I don't have any coffee. You want taters an' greens with your steak?'

'Sounds fine,' nodded Brogan. 'I guess I'll have a small beer as well.'

The bartender nodded, served him a small beer and went through to a back room. At the same time the two men at the bar wearing guns detached themselves from the others and placed themselves one each side of Brogan.

'We hear you just outdrew Arnie Semple an' Phil Grayson,' said the one to Brogan's right. Brogan took a sip of his beer and nodded. 'Now that's somethin' I sure would have liked to have seen,' continued the man. 'The name's Jess Smith, hardly an original name but it is my real name. My partner here is Gus, Gus Tranter.' Brogan nodded to each in turn. 'What do we call you?'

'Just call me Brogan,' he replied. 'Brogan

McNally.'

'McNally?' said Gus Tranter. 'I knew a McNally once, way back in Topeka. You got any kin back there?'

'None that I know of,' said Brogan. 'I'm from Seattle, but that was way back when I was a kid.'

'That's up north somewhere, ain't it?' asked Smith. Brogan nodded. 'What brings you down here?'

'My horse an' my feet,' said Brogan. 'I'm what you call a saddlebum.'

'Yeh!' sniffed Tranter, 'I can smell that.' Both men laughed. 'The thing is, since when has a saddlebum been able to outdraw anyone? Every other one I ever met had a wide yeller streak down his back. All they ever did was steal or shoot someone in the back.'

'Well, this one ain't never stole nothin' off nobody an' I ain't never deliberately shot anyone in the back unless I had to.'

'Which means that you have killed men before.' said Smith.

'I've killed my share,' nodded Brogan. 'What's it to you?'

'Nothin',' grinned Smith. 'Nothin' at all, I'm just curious about any man who outdraws Arnie Semple an' Phil Grayson.'

'Are you lookin' for work?' asked Tranter.

'Work!' laughed Brogan. 'Saddlebums don't work, I thought you knew that.'

'Well if you don't work an' you say you don't steal, how do you get by?' asked Smith.

'I gets by,' smiled Brogan. He had to admit to himself that his funds were probably at the lowest they had been for a long time. He had earned himself $200 about two months earlier when he had handed over an outlaw for the reward, but most of that had now gone. 'What kind of work are you talkin' about?'

'Somethin' that might be in your line,' said Tranter. 'Mr Feldmann is always on the lookout for men who can use a gun.'

'I ain't no hired gun,' replied Brogan, firmly.

'Suit yourself,' shrugged Tranter. 'Mr Feldmann pays well.'

'Pays well enough to get others to drive farmers off their land?' said Brogan.

'Somethin' like that,' sneered Tranter. 'There's the difference of opinion between him an' Stockwell as well, but that ain't our concern, we just do as he says an' don't ask any questions.'

'No thanks,' said Brogan. At that moment a rather fat woman arrived with a large plate of steak and vegetables which she placed on a nearby table.

'Two dollars!' she said, holding out her hand. Brogan did think about protesting at the price but decided against it, he was too hungry to haggle. He paid her the money and settled himself at the table. The two men returned to their original positions at the bar and left the stranger alone, for which Brogan was more than grateful.

About half an hour later, a tall, well-dressed man entered the saloon, looked about briefly and went to the men at the bar where the topic of conversation was obviously the stranger. After some time he came over and sat at Brogan's table.

'Can I buy you a whiskey?' he asked.

'If you want to buy me anythin' you can buy me a beer,' replied Brogan. 'Now if'n I was asked, I'd say you was Mr Feldmann an' that you just heard what happened at McGinty's an' you've come to see what I look like an' possibly to offer me a job.'

Feldmann ordered a beer for Brogan and a whiskey for himself which, Brogan noted, did not come from one of the bottles behind the bar but from a bottle under the counter.

'You learn fast,' said Feldmann with a hint of gutteral accent. 'I like men who learn fast. You are right, I am Heinrich Feldmann and like everyone else, I am fascinated by any man, saddletramp or not, who can apparently outdraw Semple and Grayson. I need men like you.'

'And just why do you need men like me?' grinned Brogan. 'I've never done no physical work in my life – not since I was a kid anyhow – an' I'm too old to start now.'

'The kind of work I had in mind would involve your gun,' smiled Feldmann. 'I have more than enough men for the other kind of work. I don't know how much you know, Mr McNally . . .' – Brogan did not normally like being called McNally but in this case he did not correct it – 'but there is a slight difference of opinion between myself and Bradley Stockwell. . . .'

'A range war,' said Brogan.

'I prefer not to call it that,' smiled Feldmann. 'The point is that I need men who can handle a gun in order to protect the other hands and to persuade certain other people, you know, make them see sense or the error of their ways.'

'Like farmers who've been here a whole lot longer'n you who should've known better,' smiled Brogan.

'For someone who has been in town for such a

short time you appear to know an awful lot,' smiled Feldmann. 'Yes, it is true, we do have some local difficulty with the farmers in Bullfrog Pass.'

'An' you an' Stockwell each want to control the pass,' said Brogan. 'It figures. Just 'cos you're rich an' own a lot of land you think you can control everythin' an' everyone. What you can't buy you take by force.'

Feldmann plainly did not like the way Brogan was talking but he smiled and looked about the room, more concerned as to whether anyone else had heard. It seemed that they had not.

'You are entitled to your opinions, of course,' he grunted. 'However, I would hold my tongue if I were you until I was more certain of the facts. Since the railroad was pushed through last year, that pass is the shortest way to it. If we don't have access through the pass it means an extra week round the mountains. We had hoped that the railroad would come through here, but for some reason they chose a more northerly route. Those farmers are now in the way, nothing more. Both Stockwell and I have offered them good prices for their land but they are very stubborn and refuse to move.'

'And you want men like me, handy with a gun, to change their minds?'

'Something like that,' admitted Feldmann. 'The important thing is not so much persuading them to sell up or move, but just who persuades them, myself or Stockwell.'

'And the one who doesn't get control has to take an extra week to drive their cattle,' nodded Brogan.

'Not necessarily,' grinned Feldmann. 'The loser also gets to use the pass – at a charge of twenty-five cents a head, and when there might be two thousand head in a drive that means a cost of five hundred dollars for the privilege.'

'An' neither of you want to pay that much,' grinned Brogan.

'Not if we can help it,' replied Feldmann. 'That's good land up there too.'

'Too good for cows,' smiled Brogan.

'Nothing is too good for cattle!' grated Feldmann.

'Sorry to disappoint you,' said Brogan, 'the answer is no, I ain't for hire an' nothin' you can do or say will alter that. Goodnight, Mr Feldmann.'

TWO

Brogan left the Black Diamond Saloon about ten minutes after Heinrich Feldmann had stormed out, obviously very displeased at having been refused, and by a saddletramp at that. The rain had ceased and there were a few people about, although there was still no obvious sign of either Semple or Grayson. However, Brogan was suddenly aware of a stocky figure bearing down on him along the boardwalk in a very determined manner.

'A word with you, stranger,' growled the man, as he sized his five feet eight inches up to Brogan's six feet three. 'I don't like folk just ridin' into my town an' causin' trouble.'

'Me cause trouble!' objected Brogan with a certain amount of justification. 'All I came in for was to get out of the rain, get me some food an' maybe a night's rest.'

'That ain't the way I heard it,' grunted the man, pulling his jacket to one side to reveal a sheriff's badge. 'I heard you pulled a gun on Arnie Semple an' Phil Grayson.'

'Is that some sort of crime?' asked Brogan. 'It was them or me; they were lookin' for a fight an' I wasn't

21

prepared to take the chance on bein' shot. Anyhow, from what I hear there ain't nobody supposed to be faster'n them two. I'm surprised they should complain to the likes of you.'

'They didn't,' grunted the sheriff, allowing his stomach to drop into its more usual place thereby increasing his girth by quite a lot and reducing his height slightly. 'It's common knowledge. I gotta admit that any man who can outdraw them two almost has my blessin', almost but not quite. The thing is I've got enough trouble already, I don't want more. When are you leavin' town?'

'I take it that is more of an order than a question,' grinned Brogan. 'It's OK, Sheriff, providin' it ain't rainin' in the mornin' I'll be on my way. I ain't lookin' for trouble.'

'You just make sure you are,' huffed the sheriff. 'So far I can deal with any trouble that crops up, but it's a fine balance and it won't take much to upset things.'

'Well I'm about to bunk down in the livery,' said Brogan, 'an' all being well you won't hear nothin' of me all night or in the mornin' for that matter.'

'I hope not,' muttered the sheriff.

Brogan touched the brim of his hat, nodded and strolled along the boardwalk in the direction of the livery and could feel the sheriff's eyes boring into his back. As he walked he was also aware that other eyes were watching him from across the street and caught a glimpse of two shadowy figures. When he reached the livery he found that there was only one oil lamp still burning but there was enough light to see what he was doing and ten minutes later he turned out that lamp.

*

About half an hour after the lamp had been turned out, the two shadows Brogan had seen earlier quietly crossed the street and, after listening at the door of the livery for some time, slowly opened it just wide enough to allow them to slip through. For a time both figures stood in the shadows, again listening before moving cautiously towards Brogan's horse and the nearby sleeping form. Suddenly, one of them lashed out with his foot, his boot sinking into the the sleeping figure, an action which was quickly repeated by the other man. . . .

'You can kick the hell out of that straw for as long as you like!' Brogan's laughing voice boomed out. 'Beatin' up on a pile of straw is just about your standard.'

'Bastard!' rasped one of the men.

'Very true,' laughed Brogan from somewhere in the darkness. 'Leastwise my ma was never married to my pa as far as I know.'

A shot suddenly rang out as one of the men fired in the imagined direction of the voice, a shot which was followed by a burst of derisive laughter. A second shot followed, another burst of laughter, and the two men fell over each other and various other objects as they scrambled for the door. Their attempted rapid exit from the livery was suddenly blocked by the stocky figure of Sheriff Sam Gorman, gun in hand.

'An' just what the hell do you two think you're doin'?' he demanded. The men very wisely did not attempt to shoot their way past the sheriff and obediently allowed him to take charge of their guns. 'You OK, McNally?' he called.

'Never better,' said Brogan, suddenly appearing alongside the men. 'Pleased to see you is on your toes, Sheriff. It looks like these fellers lost their way.'

'Well they can lose their way right into one of my cells for the night,' grated the sheriff. 'You sure you're OK?'

'Not a scratch,' Brogan grinned. 'I guess they thought they was bein' quiet but they made enough noise to wake the dead.'

'I'd say you was expectin' somethin' like this,' said the sheriff.

'I'd say you was too,' said Brogan.

'Let's just say I'd've been surprised if they hadn't tried somethin' an' the shootin' confirmed it,' said the sheriff. 'I thought maybe I was too late. Right,' you two,' he continued, 'you can spend the rest of the night in jail, for your own safety you understand, I'd hate to see you gettin' yourselves on a murder charge over one dirty saddletramp an' you spendin' the night in jail will make sure that I get a peaceful night. Now move!'

Arnie Semple looked at Brogan and sneered, 'You reckon you is pretty damned clever, don't you? Well, let me tell you somethin', McNally, or whatever your name is, you ain't left town yet.'

'And have no intention of leaving until dawn,' said Brogan. 'Have a good night's sleep. I hear tell that bunks in jail ain't so bad.'

'You should know,' grunted Phil Grayson.

'As a matter of fact I don't recall ever spendin' time in any jail,' grinned Brogan.

'An' unless you travel pretty damned fast you'll never live to try it out,' threatened Grayson.

'Enough of this jawin',' ordered Gorman. 'Move I said.'

The two men oathed some further threats and foul language but did not argue with the sheriff. To Brogan, it appeared that the sheriff was right in his assertion that for the moment he had the situation under control. Once they had gone he settled down for the night, confident that any danger had passed. He could not help but marvel at the number of times other men had tried those very same tactics and always they appeared to have assumed that the rough, blanket-covered bundle was their intended victim and he was quietly grateful for that predictable fact.

However, his sleep was suddenly and rudely interrupted as a voice called out. 'McNally, a word with you if you don't mind,' said the voice. 'I'm comin' in unarmed.'

'What the hell do you want?' grumbled Brogan. 'Can't a body get some sleep round here?'

'You can get all the sleep you want after we've talked,' said the voice. 'My name's Bradley Stockwell, I have a proposition for you.'

'My gun ain't for hire,' replied Brogan. 'I've already made that plain to your men, Semple an' Grayson, an' to Feldmann.'

'Listen to what I have to say,' said Stockwell. 'I'm comin' in an' I haven't got a gun.'

'It's a free world, so they tell me,' sighed Brogan. 'OK, come on in.'

A tall, thin figure appeared by the door and for a few moments waited until his eyes became adjusted to the darkness. 'Is there a lamp in here?' he asked.

'There should be one right by the door,' said

Brogan. 'I ain't bothered though, I can see you an' as far as I'm concerned that's all that matters.'

'Well I'd like some light, if only to see what you look like.' A match flared in the darkness and the oil lamp was lit. 'That's better,' said Stockwell, taking the lamp in his hand and moving towards Brogan whom he studied for a few moments before speaking. 'Well you sure don't look much,' he said eventually, 'but any man who can get the drop on Arnie and Phil must be something.'

'They're in jail,' said Brogan. 'For their own safety accordin' to the sheriff an' maybe he's right at that. Now what can I do for you, Mr Stockwell?'

'Yes, I know where they are,' said Stockwell, 'and it won't hurt them to stay there for a while.' He looked Brogan up and down again and smiled. 'Yes, you look and smell like a saddletramp which makes you all the more intriguing. I've come across many like you and they have always run scared.'

'Just goes to show you can't always tell,' said Brogan. 'OK, so now you've seen me, I hope you're satisfied. I don't know what else you expected, but I'll say again, I am not for hire.'

'Ten dollars a week, a dry place to sleep and all the food you can eat,' suggested Stockwell.

'For doin' what?' asked Brogan.

'Looking after my interests,' said Stockwell.

'Interests such as a range war with Feldmann an' shootin' innocent farmers off their land?' said Brogan. 'Try a hundred dollars a week.'

'No man is worth that much!' laughed Stockwell sarcastically. 'I might make an exception an' pay you twelve dollars, but for that you have to prove that you're worth it. The fact that you outdrew my two best men isn't proof enough.'

'I reckon I could pass any test you cared to put me to,' Brogan boasted, 'but that don't matter, I still ain't for hire. I ain't never hired myself out yet an' don't intend to start now.'

'You'll not get a better offer, not even from Feldmann,' said Stockwell.

'Maybe not,' conceded Brogan, 'but can't you get it into your thick head that I just ain't interested?'

'Prefer stealing for a living, do you?'

'Mister,' sighed Brogan. 'Just 'cos I'm a saddle-tramp – which I willingly admit to – don't mean that I steal for a livin'. It might come as a surprise to you but I ain't never stole nothin' off nobody in my life an' I don't care if you believe that or not.'

'I don't believe you,' said Stockwell. 'But how you made your living up till now is no concern of mine. I've seen and heard enough to know that you do have something I am willing to pay for. How about fifteen dollars?'

'We're gradually gettin' towards the hundred,' grinned Brogan.

'Fifteen dollars is my last offer,' said Stockwell.

At that moment the door opened again and Sheriff Sam Gorman entered. He seemed a little surprised to see Bradley Stockwell and looked at both men questioningly.

'Maybe I shouldn't be surprised,' said the sheriff. 'First of all Feldmann an' now you. Are you OK, McNally?'

'Couldn't be better,' said Brogan. 'It seems that just 'cos I was a bit faster on the draw than his trou-bleshooters I'm suddenly a popular feller in great demand. At least, my gun is in demand.'

'And you've just been made an offer you can't refuse,' said the sheriff.

'Somethin' like that,' replied Brogan. 'Only thing is, I have refused. I said it before an' I'll say it again, neither me nor my gun is for hire.'

'Glad to hear it,' said the sheriff. 'Don't you have anythin' better to do, Mr Stockwell?'

Bradley Stockwell sighed and shook his head. 'I've made you a good offer, McNally, think about it. I'll be in town again in the morning.'

'I've already thought about it,' smiled Brogan.

Stockwell sighed again and left the livery muttering something under his breath about not having a saddlebum refuse him.

'Neither Stockwell nor Feldmann are used to bein' turned down,' explained Gorman. 'The best thing you can do is get out of town as soon as you can, rain or no rain.'

'I'll be on my way at dawn,' assured Brogan.

'I'll hold on to Semple an' Grayson for a while,' said Gorman, 'but I have to let 'em go early since I don't have anythin' to charge 'em with.'

'I reckon I can look after myself,' said Brogan. The sheriff nodded and left, leaving Brogan wondering if he was going to have any more visitors.

Dawn and Brogan emerged at exactly the same time, Brogan leading his horse from the livery and the first rays of sunlight just catching the mountains to the west of town. Breakfast for both horse and rider invariably consisted of a couple of quick gulps of water, and this was the case as far as Brogan was concerned but his horse had fared better in finishing off some oats.

There was no sign of Frank Evans, the owner of the livery, although two store owners were even at that time in the process of removing shutters from their stores. They gave Brogan a cursory nod but otherwise ignored him and a couple of minutes later Brogan was riding slowly out of town.

It was very rare for Brogan's old horse to travel anywhere at anything more than a slow walking pace and when she did – or was forced to – it was never for very long. For this reason Brogan had often given serious consideration to getting himself a younger, fitter horse, but he had never quite got round to actually doing anything about it. The pair had developed an understanding and had been together for a great many years and she was only his second horse. He was not even certain as to how old *he* was, let alone the horse, but since it did not really matter he rarely gave it much thought. He often talked to his horse, which had never been given a name, especially when he was trying to work something out. The responses from the horse were usually in the form of nods or shaking of the head and the occasional snort and she seemed to understand what he was talking about. He had long decided that the horse probably had more sense than he had.

Other than the fact that at that moment he was heading due north, Brogan had no idea where he was going or even why. He had often been asked where he was making for or what he was looking for, to which his reply was always that he did not know but that he would know when he had found it. So far he had not found it and really doubted if he ever would.

It struck him that his present course would take

him through Bullfrog Pass and the apparently strange, religious, farming community and while he had come across many other strange communities, he was rather more interested in just what Henrich Feldmann and Bradley Stockwell were fighting about as he did not believe that it was entirely related to the farmers of Bullfrog Pass.

According to the men in McGinty's Bar, Bullfrog Pass was about five miles due north but it proved to be a very long five miles although he eventually found the ground rising towards a valley set quite high above the flat, cattle plains. At this point, owner-ship of the land either side of the approach to the valley was clearly defined by wire fences and warnings that should the traveller stray from the well-defined trail, he was in danger of being shot for trespass by men from the Stockwell ranch to his right or by men from the Feldmann ranch to his left. He had no intention of testing the accuracy of these threats and continued along the trail even though it was quite obvious that the shortest route to the pass was across a corner of Stockwell land and there were a few gaps in the fencing to tempt the unwary.

As he rode towards Bullfrog Pass, Brogan's senses, carefully honed by years of experience, were scream-ing at him that things ahead were not quite as they ought to be and he had long since learned that his senses were rarely wrong. However, he had a clear view all round of perhaps four miles either side and about half a mile to the pass but look and listen as hard as he might, he could not detect anything or anyone. He tried putting his feelings down to imagi-nation, but the nearer he got to the pass, the stronger the feeling became. He paused at the mouth of the pass, which was about two miles wide, and was still unable to see anything or anyone, but the feeling persisted.

Without really thinking, he drew his gun and slowly urged his horse forward and, as he came on to the flatter, lusher ground, he could see that there were two farms, one either side of a river which ran down the centre of the valley, both situated well up the hillside. At this point the trail divided into three, one leading up to the farm to his left and the other obviously leading to the farm to his right. The third followed the course of the river upstream which took him among some rocks which, although not very large, were certainly large enough to conceal someone. His senses were now screaming even louder.

A very slight movement to his right and the very faint click of a rifle being cocked – Brogan always maintained that he could even hear a fly land on a piece of dung 100 yards away, which was not very much of an exaggeration – and then it was a question as to who shot first. Whoever did fire the first shot was of no significance since, although he did not actually recall hearing it, there was a third shot. His vision suddenly became blurred, a searing pain filled his head and the last thing he remembered was the ground coming up to meet him. . . .

'He comes round,' announced an eerie, disembodied voice from somewhere above Brogan's body. 'I think he will live.'

'May the Lord be praised,' said another, softer voice. A blurred shape came into Brogan's view but try as he might, he could not bring the shape into focus. 'Do not struggle, brother, you are in good hands, the best there are, those of the Lord.' Brogan thought he said something but later learned that he had only been able to manage a strangled croak. 'You must sleep,' continued the soft voice. 'All will be well.' There was some talk between the two voices which Brogan could not understand and slowly he lapsed into sleep once again.

The next time he woke up, he was able to focus his eyes a little easier and this time the soft voice took on the appearance of a young woman who carefully mopped his forehead with a cool, damp cloth. He thought he had asked where he was and what had happened but it appeared that no words had left his mouth. It was some time later that that he was able to communicate with anything like any coherence.

'What happened?' he managed to croak.

'The Good Lord intervened to keep you alive, that's what happened,' said the woman. 'You have lost a great deal of blood and many other men would not have survived.' Brogan raised his hand and managed to locate the bandage around his head. 'A bullet took a piece of your skull away,' continued the woman. 'You were very lucky someone was on hand to help you. Had not help been close at hand I believe that you would have died.'

'I seem to remember somebody sayin' somethin' about bein' in the Lord's hands,' he croaked. 'I wasn't sure if I was alive or not.'

'The Good Lord ensured that we were on hand to tend you,' said the woman. 'I believe your name is Mr McNally, at least that is what Sheriff Gorman says.' Brogan attempted a nod but found the exercise much too painful and stopped.

'How long have I been here?' he managed to ask.

'Four days,' said the woman.

At first it did not register on Brogan but slowly the information sank in and he suddenly looked up, wide eyed. 'Four days! You mean I've been unconcious for *four days*!'

'This is the fourth day,' she said. 'You were very lucky; my husband and brother were close at hand when the shooting started. They saw two men running away but they did not follow, they were more concerned with you.'

'Semple an' Grayson!' muttered Brogan. 'I knew somethin' was goin' to happen an' I rode straight into it. I must be gettin' careless in my old age. You say Sheriff Gorman knows?'

'It was he who identified you,' nodded the woman. 'We abide by the law in this valley. I know most people find us strange but they seem to accept our ways and for the most part they leave us alone. My husband felt it his duty to inform the sheriff and he rode out here. The doctor from Grover has also been out to see you and it was he who operated on your head. I do not know what he did but it seems to have worked.'

'I thought you said it was the Lord who saved me!' said Brogan with a weak grin. 'Not that it matters to me who it was, I'm just grateful.'

'Even the Good Lord uses human beings to carry out His work,' she assured. 'We are all, in our way, simply His tools. Both the doctor and the sheriff are due out again today to see how you are progressing.'

'Well all I can say, ma'am, is that I'm grateful for the trouble you're goin' to, but a dirty old saddle-tramp like me really ain't worth the bother.'

'I have seen dirtier men,' she grinned knowingly. 'However, you are not dirty any more—'

'Not dirty any more! You gave me an all-over wash?' exclaimed Brogan, quite alarmed.

The woman laughed. 'You are embarrassed that I have seen your naked body? There is no need, I have seven brothers and three sons and a husband. The naked male is nothing new or exciting to me.'

'Hell, no,' muttered Brogan. 'That don't bother me at all.' He tried to look down at his body but raising his head proved too difficult. 'Did you use real soap an' hot water?'

'Of course.' She laughed again. 'Is there any other way?'

Brogan lay back, shut his eyes and groaned. 'Soap an' water!'

'There is something wrong?' she asked.

'It ain't natural!' he complained. 'Soap an hot water on a man's body just ain't natural. Last time this happened to me I caught me one hell of a cold. No, ma'am, it just ain't natural.'

'What is done is done and cannot be undone,' she said. 'That apart, I had no intention of having such a body in any of my beds. Now, do you feel well enough to eat? I have some broth which should be easy to digest.'

'Guess so,' moaned Brogan, still very upset at the thought of soap and water on his body.

A youngish man came into the room, looked at Brogan and smiled. 'It is good that you recover,' he said. 'With the Lord's help we have pulled you through. How do you feel?'

'Like I've got me a cold comin' on,' complained Brogan. The man looked at his wife questioningly.

'Mr McNally considers washing or bathing to be unhealthy,' she explained smilingly. 'Had we known this before we could have left him where he fell.'

'I wonder if the Lord would have looked upon him so kindly,' said the man.

'I hear tell that the doctor had some sort of hand in things too,' said Brogan.

'The Lord works in many ways,' said the man. 'I came to tell you that the sheriff and Doctor Hardy are near. They should be here in about ten minutes.'

Exactly ten minutes later Dr Hardy and Sheriff Sam Gorman clattered into the room.

'I'm glad to see that my efforts have not been in vain,' said the doc as he immediately set to stripping off the bandage around Brogan's head.

'These folk seem to think somebody more qualified than you did most of the work,' said Brogan.

'The Good Lord, you mean,' grunted the doctor. 'The most He did was look over my shoulder while I straightened out your skull. I don't even recall Him givin' me advice or instructions. Yeh, it looks fine, I guess you'll live. I'll ride out an' take another look in a couple of days.' He proceeded to apply a fresh dressing.

'Did you see who it was?' asked the sheriff.

'Didn't actually see anythin',' admitted Brogan. 'My guess is Semple an' Grayson; there ain't nobody else it could be.'

'That's what I would've said,' nodded Gorman. 'Only thing wrong with that is that they was in my jail until almost nine o'clock, at least an hour after you was shot.'

'Then who?' said Brogan. 'More important, why?'

'Stockwell or Feldmann?' suggested Gorman.

'Or their hired guns,' said Brogan. 'But why?'

'It don't make no sense to me either.' admitted the sheriff.

THREE

Brogan's impulse was to ride out there and then, but at his first, feeble attempt to get off the bed he ended up lying in an untidy heap on the floor and had to be lifted back on to it. After that, for one of the few times in his life, he realized that he would simply have to obey doctor's orders and leave it for at least a week before he resumed his aimless wanderings. It was pointed out to him that since he had nowhere particular to go and all the time in the world to get there, another week was not going to make much difference. The couple in whose home he now found himself seemed perfectly content with the arrangement, assuring him that his sole occupancy of the bed did not present the rest of the family with any problems, an assurance which he found hard to accept but nevertheless had to. His horse had also been taken care of and was, at that moment, in a field along with three other horses.

For the next two days he was kept in bed, only being allowed out of it to perform his natural bodily functions and even then he was carried to and from the privy by the husband and the eldest boy. His hosts were named Peter and Mary Lloyd, their three sons,

Matthew, the eldest at thirteen years, Mark, aged eleven and Luke, aged eight. The name of their next son, should they have one, was going to be John, which seemed perfectly logical.

On the second day, Doc Hardy came to examine him again and pronounced him almost completely recovered apart from the fact that he appeared to be developing a cold which Brogan almost triumphantly blamed on the fact of having been washed all over with hot water and soap. Actually Doc Hardy was inclined to agree with him, saying that since he was not used to such treatment it could have something to do with it. He was given a tonic and it was recommended that he remain where he was for a few days longer since, in his opinion, even any knock might reopen the wound in which case he, Doc Hardy, could not be answerable for the consequences. It would also allow the tonic time to act on his cold. Brogan somewhat reluctantly agreed.

The question of payment for his care and attention was brought up by Brogan, but his hosts firmly refused to accept any payment at all, claiming that they were simply doing their Christian duty. The question of Doc Hardy's fee would have to be sorted out later. Inevitably, especially when he was allowed out of bed for short spells during the day, Brogan brought up the question of both Stockwell and Feldmann and the farmers' land.

'Do you intend sellin' out?' Brogan asked Peter Lloyd.

'My people settled here long before there were any cattle or there was any town of Grover,' said Peter. 'We have far greater rights than either Stockwell or Feldmann. If they want us out they will have to murder every last woman and child.'

'They might just do that,' said Brogan.

'I do not think so,' smiled Peter. 'Those days are gone; we have laws to protect us now. Can you imagine Sheriff Gorman standing by and allowing such a thing?'

'Yeh, maybe you're right,' conceded Brogan, not entirely convinced, since he had encountered similar situations in the past and in his experience the law had either been bribed to look the other way or, in some cases, had even taken an active part in the removal of the largely innocent problem. 'There's more'n one way to make you quit though,' he pointed out. 'Barns an' homesteads have been known to suddenly catch fire or fields of crops suddenly become poisoned or burned.'

'We are prepared for such tactics,' smiled Peter. 'Besides, we have the Lord on our side.'

'I'd prefer to put my trust in my gun,' nodded Brogan. 'I don't mean no disrespect to your faith, but as far as I know prayer ain't never stopped a bullet.'

Peter smiled knowingly. 'How do you know?' he said. 'It is easy to mock. We do not mind that; invariably those who mock do not know the reality. Please do not assume that we will simply stand by and watch the destruction of our land and our way of life. There is a cupboard just inside the door, if you open it you will find six modern rifles and four handguns, perhaps not so modern but nevertheless very effective. All the farms have similar numbers of guns, but we all pray that we never have to use them.'

'I didn't have you down as fightin' folk,' said Brogan.

'Our weapons are not for fighting,' smiled Peter, 'they are for protection. There is no member of our community who will fire the first shot no matter what the provocation, but everyone, including the women and those children able to hold a gun, will not hesitate to kill anyone who seeks to kill us.'

Brogan smiled. Peter Lloyd seemed very sincere and he sensed that should the occasion ever arise, these people would give a good acount of themselves. Even so, he still had serious doubts as to whether they would be a really effective force against men who were used to and very often actually enjoyed killing. He also wondered just how good the farmers were with their guns. In his experience farmers and most town dwellers hardly knew one end of a rifle from another. Most farmers could use a shotgun quite effectively, but when tested by having to shoot another human being and not vermin or deer, their nerve more often than not failed.

'Before the railroad there was no problem,' continued Peter. 'It was hoped that the railroad would come through Grover, but for some reason it was decided to put it through further north. We are fully aware of the position in which both Bradley Stockwell and Heinrich Feldmann now find themselves. Using Bullfrog Pass would save them about a week in driving their cattle, but that is not our problem.'

'How often do they have cattle drives?' asked Brogan.

'Twice a year each,' said Peter. 'Usually about two thousand head at a time.'

'That sounds like a lot of cows,' smiled Brogan. 'When are the next drives due?'

'Sometime during the next week or two,' replied Peter. 'We do not know exactly when but we are bracing ourselves for trouble.'

'So twice a year are the only times either Stockwell or Feldmann really need to use the pass?'

'They would also like it because there is a lake about halfway which has never been known to dry out, not even in the most severe drought,' said Peter. 'The river which runs from it has been known to dry up when the water-level in the lake falls, but the lake itself never actually dries out. Most years lack of water is not really a problem though.'

'Well I hope to be on my way before the cattle drive,' said Brogan. 'In fact I think I'll give it one more day. I'm gettin' restless.'

'You are welcome to stay as long as you feel the need,' said Peter. 'I can always use an extra pair of hands on the farm.'

'Now you've just made my mind up for me,' smiled Brogan. 'Next thing'll be your wife wantin' to get me soakin' in a bath of hot water. I ain't never willingly worked for a livin' in my life, leastwise not worked with my hands labourin', an' I'm too old to start now.'

'It is rumoured that you make your living with your gun,' said Peter.

'If by that you mean I hire my gun out, then you're wrong,' asserted Brogan. 'I have occasionally had to use my gun to help folk out, folk what usually can't help 'emselves' an' I've handed the odd outlaw over to the law for the reward. I'd hardly call it a livin' though and I don't need that much money really. There ain't that much call for money out on the plains or in the desert,' he said with a wry smile. 'For

the most part I gets by without money. I don't go
hungry. I know all the things what can be eaten an'
where to look for water, which ain't always from
sources most folk even think about, even when it
looks to most folk like there ain't no food or water
about. There's nearly always somethin'.'

'Obviously you are a very resourceful man,' smiled
Peter. 'Now, since you seem so much better, would
you like to go into Grover with Mary and myself this
afternoon?'

'Sure, why not?' smiled Brogan. 'I ain't got nothin'
else to do for the moment.'

When the time came for them to leave for the
town, Mary and Peter looked oddly at Brogan.

'I see you wear your gun,' said Mary. 'Is it necessary that you do?'

Brogan looked at the belt round his waist and
suddenly felt rather ashamed. He had donned his
gunbelt out of habit, but realized that by wearing it at
that time he was, in some way, insulting his hosts. He
swiftly unbuckled it and threw it on the bed.

'Is that better?' he asked.

'Much,' smiled Mary

'I hope I don't need it,' said Brogan.

'Need it!' said Peter. 'Why should you need it?'

'Someone tried to kill me, remember,' said
Brogan.

'I do not believe they would try to do such a thing
in town,' said Mary.

'I hope you're right,' smiled Brogan. 'Somebody
wanted me dead, that's for sure, although I can't
think why, especially since the only two who might've
thought that way were in jail at the time.'

'It is certainly most strange,' admitted Peter.

*

It was a fairly slow ride to Grover, the Lloyds seeming content to let the mule hauling the wagon make his own pace, but eventually they were pulling up outside the seed merchant's store. Brogan took the opportunity to go and see Sheriff Sam Gorman who seemed surprised to see him.

'Does Doc Hardy know you're up an' about?' asked the sheriff.

'He seemed happy enough last time I saw him,' said Brogan. 'Have you had any more thoughts on who might've tried to murder me?'

'Rumour has it that Heinrich Feldmann ordered it,' said Gorman. 'That's all it is though, rumour; I ain't got one shred of evidence to go on.'

'Why should he do that?' asked Brogan.

'Seems that he wanted to stir up trouble for Stockwell,' said the sheriff. 'If the stories are right, his idea was to have you killed and set the blame on Semple an' Grayson. He knew there was bad blood between them an' you; nobody would've been surprised if either of them had tried to kill you. The one thing he didn't know though was that they were both in jail at the time.'

'That makes sense, I suppose,' nodded Brogan. 'Whatever the reason was, it seems nobody gave a shit what happened to me.'

'That's 'cos nobody does,' grinned the sheriff. 'You're just a stranger in town an' a saddlebum as well an' nobody gives a damn what happens to saddlebums. In fact most folk think that the only good one is a dead one.'

'I'm used to it,' smiled Brogan. 'Peter Lloyd tells

me there's a cattle drive due in the next week or two;
are they still intent on usin' Bullfrog Pass?'

'Two drives,' corrected Gorman. 'Stockwell is due
to start movin' his herd out on the Monday an'
Feldmann on the Wednesday. They never move out
together, even they've got more sense than that. It'd
take too long to sort out four thousand head if they
ever got mixed up. I hear tell that they're both
intendin' to use the pass.'

'And what do you intend doin' about it?' asked
Brogan.

'Nothin'!' said Gorman, firmly. 'How or where
they take their cows ain't my problem providin' no
law is broken.'

'Ain't it against the law to drive cattle through
someone else's property?'

'A moot point,' said the sheriff. 'I ain't no lawyer
an' even they can't agree. As long as nobody gets
killed an' there ain't no damage to the farmers'
homesteads, I don't really see what I can do about it.'

'I don't think the farmers are goin' to take it lyin'
down,' said Brogan.

'Don't you think I know that?' muttered Gorman.
'The trouble is they are not gunmen. They may have
guns and they might be able to use them, but I don't
think they'll be a match against either Feldmann's or
Stockwell's hired guns. If what I hear is right, nobody
on Feldmann's or Stockwell's side will fire first,
hopin' the farmers will be forced to make the first
move. If they do that then it can legally be claimed
that Feldmann and Stockwell were actin' in self-
defence.'

'Damned if they do try to stop 'em an' damned if
they don't,' said Brogan. 'I'm just glad it ain't my prob-

lem; with a bit of luck I'll be well out of here by then.'

'I wish I was goin' with you,' smiled Gorman.

'I get the impression that there's bad blood between Stockwell an' Feldmann; in fact it's pretty obvious. What's that all about?'

Sheriff Gorman sighed and nodded. 'That goes back a couple of years. Brad Stockwell blames Feldmann for the death of his eldest son. He was certainly killed by a wagon bein' driven by Feldmann and there is no question that Feldmann was drunk at the time, but then it was reckoned young Stacey Stockwell had had more than enough. Anyhow, some folk claim Stacey stepped out into the street in front of the wagon and others claim that Feldmann deliberately ran him down. Whatever the truth of it, there was never enough evidence either way. Since that time Brad Stockwell has sworn to get even with Heinrich Feldmann.'

'So Feldmann surrounded himself with armed men which made Stockwell do the same,' said Brogan. 'I've come across it before. Usin' those men against the farmers just happens to be a bonus.'

'You pick things up quick,' replied the sheriff.

'I have to,' nodded Brogan. 'My life has depended on knowin' things like that more'n once.'

Brogan left the sheriff's office and wandered over to McGinty's Bar where he was somewhat surprised to find Arnie Semple and Phil Grayson, in the company of six other men also wearing guns. All eight stared hard at Brogan as he leaned on the counter a few feet away and ordered a beer.

'I'm surprised you have the nerve to come in here,' sneered Arnie Semple. 'I hear somebody tried to kill you.'

'Yeh, somebody almost beat you to it,' smiled Brogan. 'From what I hear they was hopin' you'd get the blame. Maybe you did yourselves a favour in gettin' put in jail for the night.'

'As it turned out, maybe you're right,' said Semple. 'Me an' Phil must've been the only two in the whole territory with a cast-iron story.' He looked Brogan up and down for a moment. 'I see you ain't got your guns. Maybe that's 'cos you know you couldn't outdraw either of us again.'

'Maybe so,' Brogan agreed with a sneer. He had long since learned not to react to obvious goadings and had found that this approach very often annoyed whomsoever was goading but he could not help himself adding a further comment. 'Or maybe it's 'cos I don't need a gun to deal with the likes of you. Any man who takes to beatin' up on a pile of straw can't be too hard to deal with. After all, straw don't fight back.'

'Very funny!' growled Grayson, plainly bridling at the inference 'We'll take you on any time you're ready an' after we've finished with you you'll be just one big bandage an' not just the one round your head, that is if there's anythin' left worth bandaging.'

'I hear what you say,' said Brogan. 'I notice you say *we* an' not *me*. Anyhow, I ain't here lookin' for trouble, I just came into town for a drink.'

'Yeh,' grinned Semple, 'it must be hell livin' with all them Bible thumpers. They don't drink nothin' but water so I hear. They don't even touch coffee. No sir, they don't drink, they don't smoke an' they don't believe in fightin'. What hell of a kind of life is that?'

Brogan had not actually thought about the fact that all he had ever been given to drink by the Lloyds was water, but it was true, and he certainly could not remember seeing or smelling coffee. However, it was certainly nothing to do with him and he could live without alcohol or coffee. At that moment he was rather more interested in finding out if there were any specific plans afoot regarding the driving of the cattle through Bullfrog Pass. Not that he had any intention of being around when it did happen, but he felt duty bound to find out what he could and inform his hosts.

'I guess it must suit them,' said Brogan. 'Each man to his own, that's what I say. I hear you've got a cattle drive comin' up soon.'

'Straight through the pass!' laughed Grayson. 'When two thousand head of cattle start movin' there ain't nothin' goin' to stop 'em.'

'An' what about the farms an' the crops in the fields?'

'That ain't our problem,' said Semple. 'So a few fields of taters or turnips gets trampled into the ground an' maybe the odd buildin' gets in the way an' gets pulled down, so what? Folk here in town ain't goin' to worry too much about that. It's cattle what keeps this town goin', not taters an' turnips, an' folk know it so they ain't goin' to argue too much with either Mr Stockwell or Feldmann.'

'And if the farmers start shootin'?' asked Brogan.

All eight men laughed loudly. 'No need for anyone to worry about them,' said Semple. 'I don't reckon there'll be a single gun raised against us.'

'They do have guns,' said Brogan.

'They also have religion!' snapped Grayson. 'Anyhow, it's Feldmann who's likely to catch that kind of trouble, not us.' The men turned away and ignored Brogan and although he did try asking another couple of questions, there was no response and he had the feeling that perhaps they had already said too much.

He drank his beer and wandered slowly along the street towards the saloon frequented by men from the Feldmann ranch, the Black Diamond. Mary Lloyd was just going into the drapery store and reminded him that they would be leaving in about half an hour. He acknowledged her and said that half an hour was long enough for him to do what he had in mind.

By contrast to McGinty's Bar, the Black Diamond was almost deserted. The only other customer was an old man, who immediately tried to cadge a beer off Brogan but without success and he returned grumpily to the seat he had been occupying.

'A small beer,' said Brogan, looking round. 'Not much business about.'

'Too early,' said the bartender. 'Lookin' for anyone in particular?'

'Who said I was lookin' for anyone?' asked Brogan.

'Obvious, ain't it?' mumbled the bartender. 'First McGinty's an' now here.'

'How'd you know I was in McGinty's?'

'I saw you come in with the Lloyds, saw you cross the street an' go into the sheriff's office an' then I saw you go into McGinty's.'

'You see a lot,' smiled Brogan. 'OK, maybe I was hopin' to meet some of Feldmann's men. I just wanted to know what they were goin' to do about their cattle drive.'

'Straight through Bullfrog Pass,' replied the bartender. 'Everyone in town knows that. Even the

farmers know it an' they know damned well there
ain't nothin' they can do to stop it happenin'.
Anyhow, what concern is it of yours?'

'None, none at all,' admitted Brogan. 'I don't
intend bein' here when it happens, that's all.'

'Neither of them has said exactly when they're
movin',' said the bartender. 'But if I was you I'd make
sure I was gone by Monday, they might not agree on
much these days but they've drawn lots an' Monday
is the day Stockwell goes through. Feldmann goes
through on the Wednesday.'

'That's what I hear,' nodded Brogan. The
bartender went through to a back room and the old
man took the opportunity to approach Brogan again.

'For the price of a couple of beers, I got some
information nobody else has,' whispered the old
man.

'Regarding what?' prompted Brogan.

'Stockwell's drive an' the farmers,' croaked the old
man.

'The information first,' said Brogan. 'I'll be the
judge of what it's worth. I ain't payin' for somethin' I
already know.'

The old man thought about it for a moment and
then licked his lips and nodded. 'Stockwell ain't
goin' through on the Monday, he's goin' through on
Sunday instead on account of he knows that's the
one day when none of them stupid farmers is goin'
to lift a finger to stop him.'

'How do you know this?' asked Brogan.

'I hear things,' grinned the old man. 'Everyone
ignores Old Tom, he's daft they all say. I don't mind
if they think I'm daft or not, it gets me free beers an'
the occasional whiskey an' I do hear things which

some folk are willin' to pay for.'

'You just earned yourself a few drinks,' said
Brogan, digging into his pocket and then handing
Old Tom a dollar piece. 'Just don't tell nobody
you've told me.'

'I never saw you,' grinned Old Tom. 'Good luck,
mister.'

'It's not luck anyone's goin' to need,' said Brogan.

He was met by Peter and Mary Lloyd outside the
saloon and neither of them appeared in any way
disapproving of the fact that he had had a drink and
Mary admitted that they and most of the community
did keep the odd bottle of whiskey or brandy in the
house for purely medicinal purposes and he believed
that this was actually the case. He told them of what
he had learned regarding the cattle drives.

'We were almost certain that they were going to
push the cattle through the pass,' admitted Peter.
'We did not think that they would do so on a Sunday
though.'

'Does that make a difference?' asked Brogan,
knowing that it would. At least it would if local gossip
were to be believed.

'Sunday is the Lord's Day,' sighed Mary. 'It is
against our religion to do any work other than
preparing meals, to shoot anything, including
vermin, and it would certainly be a sin to take up
arms against a fellow man.'

'Even if your fellow man was goin' to shoot you or
wreck your house?' asked Brogan. 'I can't believe
that it could be considered a sin not to protect yourselves no matter what day it was.'

'That is our way,' replied Mary, with a simplicity
Brogan found chilling.

'We must tell the elders what you have discovered,' said Peter. 'It is up to them to decide what action to take, but it will be very difficult if not impossible to persuade them to do anything. I cannot believe that even Mr Stockwell would do something like that on the Lord's Day.'

'You'd better believe it,' said Brogan. 'While most folk believe in some form of religion they don't all think the same as you seem to. OK, so you tell these elders and then I suppose you'll just go along with what they decide?' said Brogan. 'Your farm an' the one opposite are the first in line an', from what I've seen, the closest to the river an' the likely route they'll drive their cattle. It's too rocky further up for cows so that means that there's likely to be lot of damage to your property an' your crops. Don't you care about that?'

'Of course we care,' said Peter. 'But whatever happens, the Lord is on our side. He will surely punish anyone who violates His special day, especially men like Feldmann and Stockwell.'

'I think you might get better results by usin' them rifles you got,' grinned Brogan.

'The vengeance of the Lord is far greater and much more painful than anything man can inflict,' replied Peter. 'Eternal damnation in the fires of Hell will be their lot. However, the decision is not mine to make, it is up to the elders.'

'Then let's hope, for your sake, that these elders see some sense,' said Brogan. 'I reckon Stockwell won't be too worried about eternal damnation or the fires of Hell just yet; he'll be more interested in gettin' them cows to the market in better condition an' gettin' a better price. Drivin' 'em through your

valley means that they can reach the railroad that
much quicker.'

Peter sighed and nodded. 'In many ways what you
say makes sense,' he said. 'It is most unfortunate that
for some men the Good Lord has been replaced by
another god, the desire to accumulate as much
money as possible.'

'That's the way the world goes these days,' said
Brogan, 'whether you an' your elders like it or not.'

'That does not mean we have to join them,'
replied Mary.

FOUR

Matthew, the Lloyds' eldest boy was dispatched to inform the elders that Peter and Mary, along with their guest, wanted to convene a meeting as quickly as possible, preferably that evening. Less than an hour later, the boy had returned confirming that the meeting was to take place and that they, the Lloyds, were to inform their neighbours. This time Matthew was sent across the river to two farms and the second son, Mark, sent back along the valley to two other farms.

The meeting was to take place in a hall built next to the church, itself a simple but large building standing high above everything else on what must have been the only hill in the valley. These two structures and a solitary house behind the church appeared to be the centre of community life, being the nearest thing to a town or hamlet there was, and by the time Brogan and the Lloyds arrived it seemed that everyone else had been there some time.

Brogan was surprised at just how many people there were. He later discovered that there were thirty-five farms in the valley, each housing at least four people and most considerably more. He esti-

mated that there were at least 200 people in atten-
dance, including children. The children, at least
those apparently under the age of about twelve years,
took the opportunity, with the blessing of their
parents, to play. The older children were expected to
attend the meeting but, as he later found out, were
not allowed any say in matters.

Before the meeting, Brogan was introduced to the
elders, chief of whom was the pastor and the only
man not actually a farmer. Peter Lloyd had obviously
not risen to the exalted hierarchy since he and his
wife stood obediently to one side.

'It is good to see that you are recovered,' intoned
the pastor. 'It was fortunate for you that Peter and
Mary were on hand. Have you any idea who it was?
We do, of course, hear rumours, but they can be so
unreliable.'

'Nobody has any proof just who it was,' replied
Brogan, 'so it don't really do for me to blame
anyone.'

'A noble sentiment,' beamed the pastor. 'Too
many people are prepared to point an accusing
finger without proof. Tell me, Mr McNally, are you a
regular attender at church?'

'I guess you could say that,' grinned Brogan, 'I
hear tell my mother had me christened an' I did use
a church to hide out in once in Mexico an' if there's
anyone who cares an' is around when I die, maybe
they'll get me buried proper.'

'That is not quite what I meant,' replied the
pastor, stiffly, obviously sensing that Brogan was
being flippant. 'However, it seems the way of the
world these days and certainly out here, that men are
turning away from their Maker. You and they will

most certainly regret the mistake. However, it would appear that you do care for our community since it seems you have been making enquiries on our behalf.'

'I can't say that I have any particular care for your community,' replied Brogan in all honesty, 'but Mary an' Peter have been good to me so I feel I ought to pay them back if I can and since they won't accept any money, I figure this is the least I can do.'

'Peter and Mary!' corrected the pastor. 'The man is the head of the family and must be mentioned first.' Brogan shrugged and smiled slightly. 'Now, since it appears that everyone has arrived, we must repair to the hall and listen to what you have to say. Kindly follow me.'

After being corrected as to the order of address, Brogan decided that he would not risk the wrath of the pastor further by walking alongside him. He even followed on behind a column of ten men – who proved to be the Council of Elders – and who in turn followed single file behind the pastor. Once inside the hall he was kept waiting at one side while everyone else took their seats. There then followed prayers lasting about ten minutes. Brogan stood, looked and listened, and wondered if they would go through this rigmarole if the community were under attack. He finally decided that they probably would. Eventually the prayers were over and the nod given for Brogan to join the members of the council on the platform.

'Brothers and Sisters!' intoned the pastor. 'We must all be aware that we have been promised some hard times ahead of us, the hardest being the threat to our community posed by Heinrich Feldmann and Bradley Stockwell. . . .'

The pastor droned on, apparently enjoying the sound of his own voice, telling the people something they obviously already knew until, after more than half an hour, Brogan was introduced to the audience.

'There ain't that much to tell,' said Brogan, 'most of it you know already. Both Stockwell an' Feldmann intend drivin' their cattle through this valley. Two drives of about two thousand head each an' I don't think I need tell you all that that is one hell of a lot of cows. . . .' There were reproachful looks and a few murmurs from the elders at the choice of words used by Brogan but he chose to ignore them. 'They'll just trample everythin' underfoot an' maybe even knock down any buildin's that get in their way. I know most of you are prepared to fight an' it looks like there's enough of you to win if it was just a case of fightin' men. The only trouble is it ain't goin' to make no difference as far as the cows are concerned. There are two other points you might like to consider. The first is are any of you really prepared to put a man in your sights and actually squeeze that trigger? I know most of you wouldn't think twice about killin' vermin but another human bein' is a different matter; I know, even I had to learn the hard way.'

'Feldmann and Stockwell are no better than vermin,' called a voice from the audience.

'Perhaps not,' conceded Brogan, 'but the fact is they ain't, they is flesh an' blood just the same as you an' me; they bleed when they're hurt an' their shit stinks just like yours an' mine.' There were embarrassed murmurs from the audience and disapproving coughs from the pastor and the elders but Brogan just smiled. In a way he hoped that his coarse language might shock them into doing something. He waited a moment for further comments but none were forthcoming. 'Not only that, but I have it on good authority that they will not be the ones to shoot first. They want you to do that, partly in the hope that none of you would have the nerve or that your beliefs would prevent you from firing that first shot.' There were obvious murmurings of unease raised at the prospect. 'Shootin' in retaliation or defence is one thing, but shootin' first is another. There are many men who are quite capable of doing such a thing, myself included if I have to, but I have serious doubts as to whether or not any of you could.' Again he waited for comments but there were none. 'The point about them waitin' for you to shoot first is so that they can claim they returned fire in self-defence. I think the law would be on their side and I think they might win on that score. I've been around long enough to see just how the law works in such cases.'

'Even if they were driving cattle across our land without our permission?' called another voice.

'You'd better talk to a lawyer about that,' said Brogan, 'but Sheriff Gorman seems to think you wouldn't get away with it.'

'All the lawyers are paid by either Stockwell or Feldmann,' said the voice. 'Where do we find one?'

'That's your problem,' shrugged Brogan. 'Probably you don't have time to find one.'

'They are already collecting cattle near the pass,' said another voice. 'They could push through any day.'

'I saw 'em,' admitted Brogan. 'OK, the next point is that the first drive, Stockwell's, is goin' to come through on the Sunday and not the Monday as they had planned. . . .'

'But that is the Lord's Day!' This cry came from several people. 'They can't come through here on a Sunday!' added another voice.

'They can and they most likely will,' said Brogan. 'Just 'cos you folk keep the sabbath holy don't mean that other folk do.'

'Don't they realize that they face eternal damnation?' called a female voice.

'I suggest that you try tellin' 'em,' said Brogan. 'Most folk ain't interested in what happens to their souls, an' eternal damnation is when they ain't got enough money to buy their whiskey or the saloon runs dry. They're only interested in makin' as much money as possible as quickly as possible.'

'But they can't drive their cattle through on the sabbath!' responded the woman. 'They must not be allowed to.'

'Then it's up to you to stop 'em,' said Brogan.

'We must reason with them,' she continued. 'They must be shown the error of their ways.'

'It is most unlikely that reason will prevail with such people,' interrupted the pastor. 'Unfortunately, Mr McNally is right, it is up to us to stop them. Now, are there any more questions or even suggestions as to what we do next. . . ?' He waited a moment but there was no response. 'In that case I pronounce this meeting closed. We, the elders, will deliberate and you will all be informed of our decision by midday tomorrow. I must now ask you all to join me in prayer and ask the Good Lord for guidance. . . .' The pastor intoned a prayer and the congregation dutifully responded with the necessary 'Amens'.

Suddenly, one of the children who had been allowed to remain outside rushed into the hall. 'Fire!' he shouted. 'There's a fire at the far end of the valley towards Grover, you can see the flames!'

Brogan was surprised when there was no mad rush to the doors, instead the vast majority kept to their seats and allowed the elders to vacate the platform before filing out in an orderly fashion, seemingly allowing those with property at that end of the valley, such as Peter and Mary Lloyd, to leave first.

There was no mistaking that there were flames, in fact Brogan detected three separate fires even though they must have been about four miles away. He found Peter and Mary alongside him, Mary gripping the arm of her husband and staring up at him, obviously very afraid.

'Collect the children,' said Peter. 'We must return home as quickly as possible. Brogan, it would appear that the war has started.'

It seemed that the entire population of Bullfrog Pass also had the idea of heading for the fires, almost all of those who lived nearby collecting their mules and wagons and as many buckets as they could. Those who lived at the opposite end of the valley were given lifts by others and those who lived on the way also collected buckets.

The smoke and the smell of burning filled the air as they drew closer and eventually it was plain that there were four fires, one on each of the four farms closest to the end of the valley, which included the Lloyd farm. Mercifully, or so almost everyone thought, it was not the houses which were on fire but the barns, although apart from some hay and other fodder, these normally contained a great deal of valuable equipment.

The other farmers and even the pastor needed no instructions, human chains were quickly formed between river and barns and between water pumps and barn, small children also playing their part in running back with empty buckets to the source of water.

However, as far as Brogan could see, they were fighting a losing battle and he eventually left the line he was in and sought out Peter Lloyd and the pastor – who happened to be in his line.

'Let 'em burn,' suggested Brogan. 'Just make sure the flames don't spread.' He pointed to the roof of the house. 'There's burnin' debris startin' to fall on the house now. Get a ladder, get a couple of folk on the roof an' get the rest to pass water up the ladder. The important thing is to keep the roof as wet as possible.'

'I'll get someone to go to the other farms and get them to do the same,' gasped the pastor. 'You're right, we can't get close enough to the barns to do much good.'

'It might be an idea to get somebody to go an' call out Sheriff Gorman,' said Brogan. 'He might have some idea who did this.'

'Stockwell or Feldmann,' growled Peter.

'Sure to be one of 'em,' agreed Brogan. 'The question is which?'

Matthew Lloyd was once again despatched and although he seemed reluctant to leave the fire, he also felt very important at being chosen to deliver the message.

The chains were reformed and soon water was

being poured over the roofs of all the farmhouses and by the time Sheriff Gorman and Matthew Lloyd returned almost two hours later, all four fires had subsided and the lines had been moved yet again to start dousing the remaining fires now that the danger of hot debris setting fire to the houses had passed.

When Sheriff Gorman arrived at the Lloyd farm, Brogan guessed that it must have been about two o'clock in the morning, although nobody, not even the children, appeared tired.

'Any ideas who did this?' asked Brogan.

'Ideas? Yes. Proof? No,' replied the sheriff. 'I've been expectin' somethin' like this to happen for several months now'. I'm just surprised it didn't happen sooner. Young Matthew tells me you were all up at a meetin' up at the hall.'

'For what it was worth,' nodded Brogan. 'If prayer an' words could solve anythin' there'd be no problem.'

'Someone must've known,' said the sheriff. 'They knew they wouldn't be seen.'

'What do you intend doin' about it?' asked Brogan.

'What the hell can I do?' muttered Gorman. 'Nobody sees nothin'; nobody hears nothin' nobody can say if it was Feldmann's men or Stockwell's. The one thing I ain't got is a crystal ball. All I can do is go through the motions of askin' around but I know I'll be laughed off both ranches and in the absence of proof I can't say that I blame them.'

'The question is how did they know?' said Brogan. 'I suppose it could have been pure chance.'

'Excuse me, sir,' interrupted Matthew. 'But when I

went to tell the Flemings across the river about the meeting, there was a man riding through the valley towards Grover. He asked me what I was in such a hurry about and I must have told him something, but I don't think I mentioned you, Mr McNally.'

'He probably gathered that everyone was being summoned to the meeting,' said Brogan. 'It's OK, son, it ain't your fault. Would you recognize the man again?'

'I . . . I'm not certain,' replied Matthew. He thought for a short time 'No, sir, I don't think I could. I sure wouldn't like to blame someone when I wasn't sure.'

'It don't matter, son,' smiled Brogan. 'OK, Sheriff, I guess it's up to you now. Me? The quicker I'm out of here the better I'll be pleased.' That might have been Brogan's sentiments for the sheriff's benefit, but privately he knew that he was now too deeply involved with these people to just ride away from their troubles. If nothing else he knew that he had to try and help.

Sheriff Gorman made a tour of the other farms to make sure that all was in order before returning to Grover. At about the same time, most of the farmers also started to drift back to their own farms, assuring the four affected farmers that they would all be along to pull down the old barns and erect new ones. Erecting new barns was always a great social occasion at which the owner of the new barn provided food, and a barn dance was organized. In this case, four new barns meant four, rare days of festivities. Brogan made the observation that if the cattle drives went through there might be occasion for even more barn dances in the wake of the herds

Mary and the boys were sent to bed by Peter who insisted on keeping watch over the dying embers. Brogan stayed with him for a short time but eventually he too retired to bed.

Despite going to bed so late, everyone was up and about at dawn and the first thing they did was look at what was left of the barn. There was not much still standing, a few charred uprights and half a burned wall. There were some bales of hay still smouldering and a great deal of blackened, fallen timber and some farm implements, the wooden handles now little more than charred stumps. It appeared that Peter Lloyd had sat up all night, but he seemed to have gone past the need for sleep.

Brogan picked through the remains of some saddles and harness and smiled ruefully. 'I guess I need a new saddle,' he said to Peter. 'Only trouble with that is they're darned expensive an' I don't have that kind of money.'

Peter smiled and shook his head. 'There, you are once again most fortunate, Brogan,' he said. 'Your saddle was not in the barn. . . .' He pointed at a small shed behind the house. 'All your belongings were stored in there, including your rifle. The remains of the saddles you see belonged to us, but fortunately we rarely used them, so it is no great loss. Nearly all of our journeys are undertaken as a family so we use a wagon on most occasions. When the boys do ride they tend to ride everywhere bareback; for some reason they prefer it.'

'That's a relief,' admitted Brogan. 'Not that it makes your loss any the less an' it sounds very selfish of me. Your loss is probably greater than mine would've been. It looks to me like you've lost a lot of tools an' things.'

'Such things are relative,' said Peter ruefully pulling on the handle of a plough and smiling as the wooden remains simply crumbled in his hand. 'Your possessions are of as much importance to your way of life as these tools are to us. They can be repaired and fortunately it would appear that there is no damage to the metal. It will be a new experience for the boys, an experience that perhaps would have been better not to have to go through, but they have to learn how to work wood and repair tools sometime. I wonder if Sheriff Gorman has had any success in finding out who is responsible?'

'I wouldn't like to bet on it,' said Brogan. 'Maybe I'll ride into Grover an' find out, unless you want me to help out here.'

'It is just a matter of salvaging what we can,' said Peter. 'We can manage.'

At that moment three men rode up to the farm on a buckboard, the pastor and two of the elders. They each acknowledged Brogan and Peter and, after climbing off the buckboard, stood around silently apart from 'Tut-tutting' and stroking their chins. Eventually the pastor turned to Peter.

'It is the same at the Grahams',' he said. 'Almost total destruction. The problem was that everything was so dry, it has been about five weeks since we had any rain.'

'But it was throwin' down a real gale when I arrived in Grover,' said Brogan.

'That was in Grover,' smiled the pastor. 'It is not uncommon for there to be rain there and not here and sometimes the other way round. Very often the clouds are driven across the plains and are turned away by the hills. I have seen floods at Grover and near drought here.'

'I'll take your word for it,' nodded Brogan. 'I thought of goin' into Grover to see if Sheriff Gorman has found anythin' out, which I doubt.'

'As do we all,' sighed the pastor. 'I fear that there is little anyone can do but we must not allow either Feldmann or Stockwell to believe that they have beaten us into submission. Once we do that we might as well all leave Bullfrog Pass.'

'Have the elders decided on what to do?' asked Peter.

'Unfortunately we have not, as yet, had time to deliberate,' replied the pastor. 'However, what has happened puts a very different light on our deliberations. It is not just the four farms which were attacked last night we have to think about, we have responsibilty for the greater community. We have convened a meeting for midday and our decision will be made known to you soon after.'

'May the Good Lord guide you,' said Peter. 'Now, I am sure my wife, Mary, will be able to find you some breakfast.'

'Most welcome,' nodded the pastor. 'We all left without eating.'

'I'll go and tell her,' said Peter. He went off to the house leaving everyone looking thoughtfully at the still smouldering embers.

'As a man of the world, Mr McNally,' said the pastor, 'what would you do under these circumstances? I am the first to admit that we have been rather insulated from the world at large. It has been our choice, I know, but I do not believe that any of us

would wish it otherwise. However, there are times
when the views of an outsider may well be of use;
even the elders do see the advantage of a fresh pair
of eyes from time to time. I have no doubt that Peter
has already told you that we are well armed and that
every last man, woman and child would be prepared
to fight for our survival should it prove necessary.'

'He has,' said Brogan. 'I hear all the farms have
some modern weapons.'

'Most have,' nodded the pastor. 'There are some,
particularly of the older generation who have lived
through hard times in the early days, surviving
attacks by the Indian tribes. They alone have experience of killing their fellow men, although at the time
the Indians were considered little more than vermin
or at the most primitive savages. The thing is, as you
said in your address to the meeting last night, those
few apart, like you, I do not believe that most would
be able to actually kill another man, be he Indian or
gunman for either Feldmann or Stockwell. However,
that does not answer my question, Mr McNally.'

'What would I do?' Brogan smiled and shook his
head. 'You're askin' the wrong man, Reveren', I've
been a drifter since I was sixteen an' that's more
years than I care to remember. I ain't never owned
no property apart from a horse, saddle an' my guns
in my life an' I ain't never wanted to. If I meet problems I simply move on, but I guess that's just what
Stockwell an' Feldmann would want you to do.'

'I sense that things are not quite as simple as you
make them appear,' smiled the pastor. 'Had you
been nothing more than another drifter – or saddletramp as they call them – I do not believe that you
would have done the things you have done.'

'I ain't done nothin',' Brogan pointed out.

'But you have,' said the pastor. 'You have shown that you care, albeit in a small way, by making the enquiries you have made and for telling us about them.'

'That was because of what Peter and Mary Lloyd did for me,' said Brogan. 'If it hadn't been for someone tryin' to kill me I wouldn't be here now, I would've ridden through your valley and been maybe a hundred miles away by now.'

The pastor smiled, placed his hands together and touched his lips with his fingertips and raised his eyes to the sky. 'I know that you will not accept what I say, Mr McNally,' he said, 'but it is my belief that what happened is the will of the Lord. He arranged for you to be shot and ensured your survival. I believe He has chosen you to lead us in our times of trouble.'

'Well He ain't never told me nothin' about it,' said Brogan. 'As far as I'm concerned I'm only here because I outdrew someone who was suppose to be the fastest gun the territory or because someone else heard about it an' used me to try an' stir up trouble.'

'I told you that you would not accept what I say,' nodded the pastor. 'Very well, Mr McNally, you have your view and I have mine.'

'If this God of yours is so darned powerful,' said Brogan, 'why don't He just solve the problem for you? Why don't He simply force Feldmann an' Stockwell to drive their cows round the long way?'

'It is not for us to question His ways,' said the pastor. 'You said that you were riding into Grover to see if the sheriff has discovered anything. That does not seem to me to be the actions of someone who does not care.'

'I could just ride out here an' now,' Brogan pointed out.

'But will you?' smiled the pastor.

FIVE

After breakfast, Brogan found his saddle and half an hour later was riding out towards Grover, which was supposed to be no more than five miles away although it certainly seemed a lot further. If he was to guess he would have said about ten miles. However, whether it was five miles or ten miles was of no importance as far as he was concerned and probably not that important for the citizens of Grover or the farmers of Bullfrog Pass. Eventually Brogan was riding up the main street of the town towards Sheriff Sam Gorman's office and appeared to be attracting some interest.

'They must've heard what happened,' he said to the sheriff, after closing the door to the office and looking out of the window at several people who were gathering in the street.

'They heard,' said the sheriff. 'The only ones who haven't heard are those in the cemetery.'

'Have you found out who did it?'

'Nope!' shrugged Gorman. 'The only thing I know for certain is that it was either Stockwell or Feldmann. I was goin' to ride out an' talk to them, not that it will do much good, but I have to be seen to be doin' my job. I hear that both will be in town later this mornin' so I thought I'd save myself a journey. How are things up at the pass?'

'Pretty much as you might expect,' replied Brogan. 'Four barns completely destroyed along with a whole lot of tools an' things. Peter Lloyd reckons most of his tools can be saved and repaired though. Any news on when they're goin' to start the cattle drives?'

'Next week, from what I hear,' said the sheriff. 'That's what the meetin' up in the valley was about, wasn't it? What are they goin' to do about it?'

'Fight,' smiled Brogan, not entirely certain whether or not they would but he thought that somehow the prospect might just deter Feldmann and Stockwell.

'That's all I need!' sighed the sheriff. He looked at Brogan and laughed. 'Before you turned up I thought I had everythin' under control. Maybe I was foolin' myself, I don't know, but suddenly you ride into town an' everythin' starts blowin' up in my face.' He laughed again. 'Sure, I know it was goin' to happen anyway an' maybe I'm just bein' stupid in thinkin' that it was you who put a jinx on it, almost like you was sent to stir things up.'

'I have that effect on people sometimes,' Brogan smiled. 'The pastor even thinks I was sent by God to sort things out for them.'

'The Devil more like,' grinned Gorman.

'Now that I could believe,' laughed Brogan. 'Maybe I'll suggest that to the pastor; he might not want me to help if he believed that.'

'I know I don't have much time for their ways,' said the sheriff, 'but they never gave me no trouble an' I guess they do have prior claim since they were here long before any of us. But I can't help thinkin' that unless they move with the times they're just stokin' up a whole load of trouble for themselves.'

'I ain't a religious man,' said Brogan, 'but as far as I see it they've got every right to do what they like how they like providin' it don't hurt nobody else.'

'You can see Feldmann's an' Stockwell's point though,' said Gorman. 'A week extra can cost them a whole lot of money in terms of poorer cattle.'

'Sure, I see their point,' agreed Brogan, 'an' I reckon if they was to talk to each other they could come to some agreement.'

'Both Feldmann and Stockwell offered to buy them out,' said Gorman. 'I can't say if it was a fair offer or not, but the farmers just weren't interested which made both the ranchers more determined than ever. Do you intend stoppin' to help 'em?'

'I wish I knew the answer to that,' sighed Brogan. 'On the one hand there's more'n enough of 'em to sort things out for themselves, on the other hand they ain't fighters in the sense of bein' prepared to kill for their land. Die for it, maybe, an' I'm afraid that's just what will happen.'

'Which means that you're goin' to help,' said Gorman.

'Maybe,' nodded Brogan, even then not prepared to totally commit himself. 'I'll hang around for a while to see how things go.'

With little else to do, Brogan ambled along the street to the Black Diamond Saloon where he found five people lounging about. Immediately four of the five hastily drank what they had and clattered out of the saloon, obviously not prepared to remain in his presence. The fifth man turned out to be Old Tom and without being asked Brogan bought another beer and set it down in front of the old man.

'Could be the last you'll ever buy anyone,' muttered the old man as his fingers eagerly clasped the glass just in case Brogan should change his mind.

'Meanin' what?' asked Brogan, straddling a chair and resting his chin on the back of it.

'Meanin' that certain folk round here are determined to see you dead,' responded Old Tom.

'Like who?' asked Brogan, already knowing the answer.

'Don't reckon I need to spell it out,' slurped old Tom through his beer.

'Probably not,' agreed Brogan. 'Does that apply to Stockwell as well?'

'Sure does,' nodded Old Tom. 'You ain't safe in here or McGinty's.'

'An' that's why those folk left when I walked in?' asked Brogan.

'They don't want to get in the way of any stray bullets,' said Old Tom. 'You can bet your life that word is already on its way to both ranches that you're here.'

'Then maybe I'd better leave before they arrive,' smiled Brogan. 'I've got just one thing against doin' that, an' that is I ain't never run scared in my life.'

'I'd say it wasn't a case of runnin' scared,' said Old Tom. 'I'd say it was a case of self-preservation. Men like Arnie Semple an' Phil Grayson ain't stupid, they know you ain't no ordinary saddlebum, they've already seen how fast you are. Besides, they never hunt alone, always in pairs or a pack. Same goes for Jess Smith an' Gus Tranter, Feldmann's men, an' I'd say this was one occasion when they act together. You don't stand a chance, Mr McNally. Take my advice, for what it's worth an' get the hell out of here an' forget your pride.'

'An' what's brought about this sudden dislike of me,' asked Brogan. 'I know Semple an' Grayson didn't like what happened but I got the impression that nobody really cared or were bothered to put themselves out to kill me.'

'It ain't so much them, leastways not as far as Smith an' Tranter are concerned, but they're under orders from Feldmann,' said Old Tom. 'Seems like they know you've teamed up with the farmers an' they don't like it. Without you the farmers would be no trouble; they ain't fightin' men, but with you leadin' 'em they think that maybe they could be organized.'

'I'm flattered that they should think so highly of me,' grinned Brogan. 'They know more'n I do, I ain't decided what I'm goin' to do.'

'You'll stay,' said Old Tom. 'It don't need no crystal ball to tell that, although why you should be so concerned is beyond the likes of me.'

'Maybe it's 'cos I don't like the idea of someone tryin' to kill me,' replied Brogan, touching the bandage round his head. 'If they hadn't done that I'd probably have been a couple of hundred miles away by now.'

'That was their mistake,' nodded Old Tom.

Suddenly Brogan laid his hand on Old Tom's shoulder and touched his lips with his other fingers, indicating that Tom should keep quiet. 'We've got company an' that means trouble,' he said quietly, as his ears picked up the slightest creak of a floorboard outside the door and his senses told him all was not right. Old Tom raised his eyes and then looked at Brogan questioningly.

'Don't see nobody,' he said.

'You'll see,' said Brogan, not moving. 'Two men, maybe three, an' since this is Feldmann's bar I'd say it was Smith an' Tranter.'

'What you goin' to do?' whispered Tom.

'You'll see,' muttered Brogan again as he changed position slightly.

Brogan's prediction of trouble proved very accurate as two men suddenly burst into the room, guns in their hands. . . .

It was Old Tom's boast that even though he was considered stupid, he missed nothing, but in this case even he had to admit that he was uncertain as to what happened next.

What did happen was that Brogan suddenly threw himself sideways, rolled across the floor and bounced to his feet, his gun firing as he did so. Two shots, one each from Smith and Tranter, thudded harmlessly into the floor but Brogan's first shot struck home and Smith crumpled to the floor. A second shot from Tranter missed its target and shattered a mirror behind the counter as Brogan suddenly crouched and fired again. This time Tranter reeled round, dropped his gun and he too fell to the floor. Brogan slowly stood up as if expecting someone else to burst into the room, but nobody did. He stood over the two men, his gun still at the ready and using the toe of his boot, turned Smith over. He was still alive and appeared to have been shot in the chest. Tranter lay on his back, his legs moving as he groaned. His wound appeared to be in his shoulder.

'I guess you'll live,' he sneered at Tranter. 'Tom, go get Doc Hardy to look at this one. He's still alive but he took it in the chest.'

By that time the pounding of feet could be heard on the boardwalk but it appeared that nobody was prepared to enter the saloon. The bartender had ducked under his counter as soon as Smith and Tranter had burst into the room and was just then nervously emerging from cover. Old Tom had not moved and Brogan was just about to tell him once again to find Doc Hardy when Sheriff Sam Gorman came into the room, gun at the ready. He was plainly very surprised to see the bodies of Smith and Tranter and appeared equally surprised to see Brogan still alive.

'What the hell happened?' he demanded.

'They happened,' said Brogan, smiling slightly and returning his gun to its holster. 'I was just havin' me a drink when they burst in an' tried to kill me.' He shook his head as a pain shot through it. He realized that the sudden movement had been a little too much. 'Go get Doc Hardy to look at me, I don't give a damn about them, but my head feels like it's burstin'.'

'Is that right, they tried to kill him?' Gorman demanded of both Old Tom and the bartender, ignoring Brogan's request. Both men nodded and Old Tom added that Brogan seemed to know they were there. The sheriff looked at Brogan, his head tilted slightly in a questioning manner.

'I hear things,' said Brogan but did not elaborate further.

There was no need for anyone to call Doc Hardy, word had already reached him via the crowd now assembled outside and he pushed his way through into the saloon where he first of all looked briefly at the bodies on the floor and then at Brogan who, by that time, had sat down and was slumped over a table.

'Get that man over to my office at once!' he ordered Sheriff Gorman, indicating Brogan. 'I'll be over there shortly. I'll look at these two here.' Sheriff Gorman did not argue with the doctor and he helped Brogan outside where he instructed another man to take him to the doctor's office. Doc Hardy knelt down and examined Jess Smith. 'He'll live,' he announced. 'I don't think the bullet touched any vital parts. It's still in there though; I'll have to take it out.' He turned his attention to Gus Tranter and again pronounced that he would live and that the bullet had passed through his shoulder and that all that could be done was to dress it.

At that moment both Heinrich Feldmann and Bradley Stockwell arrived from opposite directions, Stockwell accompanied by Arnie Semple and Phil Grayson. Feldmann asked the bartender what had happened and it seemed that he had witnessed quite a lot from the floor behind the counter. Stockwell appeared reasonably pleased, apart from admitting to Sheriff Gorman that he would have preferred it had Brogan been killed.

'Remember who pays your salary, Sheriff,' Stockwell whispered. 'It would be very convenient if this McNally was to spend time in jail on an attempted murder charge.'

'It was self-defence,' protested Gorman. 'I ain't got

no cause to arrest him.'

'I know that,' hissed Stockwell, 'but maybe you're not too sure of the facts and need time to sort things out. All that's needed is another four days.'

'Next Sunday!' said the sheriff. 'You're still sure about goin' through on Sunday then?'

'I'm doing you a favour, Sam,' grinned Stockwell. 'Any other day and the farmers just might try to stop us and there could be a lot of unnecessary shooting and probably a few deaths. We know enough about them to know that they wouldn't lift a finger to help themselves on a Sunday.'

The sheriff sighed and shook his head. 'McNally's over at Doc Hardy's place right now. It seems that what he just did shook up his head. I can't do nothin' unless the doc pronounces him fit enough.'

'Then just make sure he isn't fit enough to do anything!' Stockwell hissed again. 'Oh, and about Sunday; you haven't been fishing for a long time, it could be a good day for fishing. I hear tell there's a couple of big ones out in Lizard Creek.'

'I'll think about it,' muttered Gorman.

In the meantime, Jess Smith was taken across to Doc Hardy's office and Gus Tranter's shoulder was cleaned and patched. Heinrich Feldmann immediately interrogated Tranter and was plainly displeased. Sam Gorman did not help matters when he informed Feldmann that he might have to consider an attempted murder charge against both Smith and Tranter.

'I'd think seriously before I did anything about that if I were you,' Feldmann growled in reply. 'I helped make this town and this territory what it is and you should remember that. McNally is nothing more than a saddletramp, even he admits that, and nobody cares what happens to saddletramps.'

'Maybe I should consider chargin' you as well,' said the sheriff. 'It was your men, acting under your instructions who tried to kill McNally.'

'And with you turning a blind eye,' reminded Feldmann. 'We had an agreement, remember?'

'You had the agreement,' replied Gorman, 'I didn't agree to nothin'. All I said was that if I didn't happen to be around there was probably nothin' I could do. Well, it looks like things've backfired on you. You were warned that McNally was no ordinary saddlebum and I did say I thought you were bein' stupid in havin' your men kill him.'

'You agreed not to be around,' snarled Feldmann. 'I had witnesses already primed.'

'I didn't agree to nothin',' snarled the sheriff. 'All I said was—'

'I know what you said, Sam,' hissed Feldmann. 'Maybe this town will be lookin' for a new sheriff soon.'

'If you can find anyone fool enough to do the job,' grunted Gorman.

'I don't think you did any damage,' said Doc Hardy as he examined Brogan's wound. 'I did tell you to take it easy though. If you go around doing things like that you must expect it to hurt.'

'Doin' things like what?' asked Brogan.

'Like throwing yourself all over the floor,' replied the doc. 'At least that's what I heard from Old Tom.'

'And you believe everythin' he says?' smiled Brogan.

'I believe anything that man tells me,' said the doc.

'He acts stupid but that's all it is, an act. Believe me, that man misses nothing and he doesn't tell lies.'

'I believe you,' said Brogan. 'Anyhow, what the hell was I supposed to do, stand there an' let 'em shoot me?'

'It might save everybody a lot of trouble if you did,' grunted the doc.

'Includin' the farmers?'

'Including the farmers,' nodded the doc. 'It might save them a lot of heartache and trouble if they just allowed the cattle through. They can pick up the pieces later.'

'Until the next time and then the next,' said Brogan. 'How are Smith and Tranter?'

'As if you care!' laughed the doc. 'Smith needs a bullet taking out of his chest. In fact I'm about to operate on him any moment now. Tranter will be nursing a sore shoulder for a while, but that's all.'

'I must be gettin' senile,' grunted Brogan. 'They should both have been dead.'

'I wondered about that,' smiled the doc, as he replaced the bandage. 'Maybe you're getting too old for the kind of business you're in.'

'I'm too old to quit now,' said Brogan. 'And I don't know no other life an' I could no more settle down anywhere than fly to the moon. No thank you, Doc, a drifter I've always been and always will be. Maybe I should get in a bit of practice with my gun though.'

'The older we get, the slower we get,' smiled the doc. 'Remember that and don't try to act as if you were still in your twenties. You'll be OK, but be careful – I don't mean with your head – I mean watch Sam Gorman. He's been ordered to make sure you don't interfere with what happens on Sunday. I know he doesn't like the idea of Stockwell and Feldmann doing what they intend to, but he also knows that between them they control the entire territory, including him. They could soon arrange to vote him out of office if they wanted to and he knows it.'

'Thanks for the warnin',' said Brogan. 'I guess I have to watch my back and both sides from now on. Did you say the drive starts on Sunday?' The doc nodded. 'Then I'd better get back an' tell 'em.'

Doc Hardy pressed Brogan's shoulder. 'I wish you luck, my friend. I am probably about the only person in Grover who can honestly say that I don't depend on Feldmann or Stockwell in some way. Personally I like the farmers. I don't necessarily agree with everything about their religion but at least they're honest and decent people and they pay their bills on time.'

'Oh.' Brogan grinned sheepishly. 'I guess I owe you. How much?'

'Nothing,' grinned the doc. 'The community have already paid. In fact they overpaid me and told me it was for future treatment.'

'I didn't know that,' said Brogan. 'They must've known somethin' about me needin' more treatment, certainly more'n I did.'

'Well you know now,' said the doc. 'Just make sure they don't come off the worst.'

'I wasn't too sure if I was goin' to hang about an' help or not,' said Brogan, 'but partly because I object to anyone tryin' to kill me – an' this is the second time – an' partly because I don't really think they would know what to do, I'll do my best.'

'That's all any man could ask,' smiled the doc. 'It's a pity they can't come to some agreement with Feldmann and Stockwell though.'

*

Brogan and Sheriff Sam Gorman met as Brogan left Doc Hardy's office. The sheriff was obviously ill-at-ease. He looked at Brogan almost apologetically and then looked about nervously.

'I . . . er . . . I reckon I have to arrest you on an attempted murder charge, McNally, leastways until I sort out exactly what did happen.'

'You mean until after Sunday when Stockwell drives his cows through Bullfrog Pass,' said Brogan. The sheriff shuffled uneasily. 'Go ahead, Sheriff,' Brogan invited. 'Do you reckon you could take me?' His hand dropped threateningly to the handle of his gun. If the sheriff had insisted on arresting him, he certainly would not have resisted, but he was banking on the sheriff not knowing that fact.

'Kill me an' you'd be on the run for the rest of your life,' warned Gorman.

'How long I was on the run would be of no interest to you if you were dead, would it, Sheriff? I know you've been ordered to make sure I don't interfere in what happens on Sunday, but ask yourself whose side you're on, Stockwell's or the law? I'm goin' back to Bullfrog Pass and don't try to stop me.'

'Get out of here!' growled the sheriff, glancing about to see if anyone was watching. 'Get out an' don't come back into town or I just might have to arrest you.'

'I'm goin',' grinned Brogan.

He crossed the street to the Black Diamond where he had tethered his horse and was confronted by Heinrich Feldmann and an ashen-looking Gus Tranter, who now had his arm in a sling to take the weight off his shoulder. For a moment they stopped and stared at each other.

'You got lucky again,' grated Feldmann. 'The next time you'll find your luck has deserted you, I promise you that.'

'You can try me now if you like,' invited Brogan. 'I still feel lucky.'

'You would like that wouldn't you, McNally?' hissed Feldmann.

'Not particularly,' replied Brogan. 'I couldn't care less what happens to you or how it happens.'

'I am not a gunman,' said Feldmann, 'I freely admit as much, but I am rich enough to hire men to do such things for me.'

Brogan laughed and looked Gus Tranter up and down. 'Then it looks like you've been wastin' your money, don't it?'

'You can laugh now, McNally,' said Feldmann, 'I wonder how much you'll laugh when another bullet smashes that stupid head of yours.'

'I didn't laugh the first time,' said Brogan. 'I don't know who it was, but I have my ideas an' I intend payin' 'em back – with interest.' He pushed past the two men and mounted his horse and he was no sooner in the saddle than his gun was once again in his hand as he saw Feldmann force Tranter's arm down. 'Very wise,' nodded Brogan, 'I need a bit of target practice an' it might've been that you'd've been in the way. I'd tell your men to stick to herdin' cows if I was you, at least they can't shoot back.' He rode out of Grover knowing that dozens of eyes were watching his every move, but he was well used to such things and in some perverse way actually enjoyed being the centre of attention.

SIX

'So there you have it,' said Brogan. 'Stockwell intends goin' through this Sunday. It's up to you what happens next. You can stand an' fight or you can watch a whole load of cows trample everythin'.'

He was addressing a hastily convened meeting of the elders who had been summoned to the Lloyds' farm. At first there was no response as they all looked at each other, nobody prepared to suggest what to them was unthinkable – that they take up arms on the sabbath. Eventually the pastor broke the silence.

'The Lord's day is holy,' he said, 'Even under these extreme circumstances our faith must hold. I shall go and talk to Mr Stockwell and get him to see our point of view, even though I fear that I shall be wasting my time.'

'Nothin' more certain,' nodded Brogan, 'and assumin' he won't listen – which he almost certainly won't, if you don't act to protect yourselves this time, you're finished. What happens the next time and the time after that? I'll tell you what'll happen. They'll just ride over you whenever it suits 'em an' pretty soon your folk'll've had enough an' they'll start leavin'. Is that what you want? I've been thinkin' though an' maybe there is a way out. It's a slim chance but the only one you've got.'

'We are prepared to listen to any suggestion,' said one of the elders, 'providing it is legal and does not compromise our beliefs.'

'Oh, I reckon it's legal all right,' said Brogan. 'I don't know if it goes against your beliefs or not an' frankly I don't give a damn. When I first came into Grover, I found out that Feldmann an' Stockwell want control of Bullfrog Pass, mainly for their own use but not entirely. It was suggested that whoever did control the pass would allow the other to drive his cattle through on payment of twenty-five cents a head. . . .' The elders murmured and looked at each other and at the pastor. 'If they take two thousand head through that means five hundred dollars. That don't sound like a bad sum to me. Now, since you control the pass, why don't you offer to let the cows through at the same charge? Two cattle drives of two thousand head apiece, that's four thousand cows an' at twenty-five cents a head that's a thousand dollars. A thousand dollars which could be used to compensate for any damage and even leave some over to do what you like with.'

'That might not cause too much of a problem for some,' objected one of the elders. 'but to others it most certainly will be, particularly those, like me, who have farms at the head of the valley. It narrows after the lake and that many cows would be certain to cause a great deal of damage. There is also the question of the three farms surrounding the lake. They are close to it and the land along which the cattle would have to be driven is some of the most fertile and at this time of year would result in a great loss of crops.'

'But at least you would be paid for that loss,' reminded Brogan. 'I don't know anythin' about farm prices or just how much you sell, but a thousand dollars to be shared out twice a year ought to compensate.'

'It is not just a question of money,' objected the elder again. 'It is a question of our rights, our ownership, our way of life.'

Brogan smiled. 'I ain't defendin' Stockwell or Feldmann,' he said, 'but I reckon that's just how they see things. Remember, they're in business just like you are. You sell your crops an' you even use the railroad to transport 'em. Like it or not, they do have a point about takin' the shortest route to the railroad an' gettin' a better price.'

'But we have prior claim on the land,' objected the elder.

'I seem to remember somethin' in the Bible about about lovin' thy neighbour,' smiled Brogan. 'It just strikes me your attitude ain't very lovin'.'

'I do not think we require a lecture on the Holy Book from someone who admits that he has never been to church,' muttered the elder.

'It is true that the money would pay for any loss or damage,' interrupted the pastor, 'and it is also true that we are hardly in a position to prevent the cattle being driven through, so I would suggest' – he addressed the elder who had objected – 'that it would be better to be paid for the damage.'

The elder sighed and slowly nodded his head. 'Should all else fail I suppose we must agree. As you say, it is not ideal but it would be better than nothing.'

'I have heard the suggestion before,' responded

the pastor, 'and I must agree that it is not without some merit, but I have serious doubts as to whether or not either Mr Stockwell or Mr Feldmann would agree.'

'Have you put it to 'em?' asked Brogan. There was an embarrassed silence. 'Well, unless you do suggest it, you certainly won't know one way or the other.'

'Brothers,' sighed the pastor, 'Mr McNally is quite correct. It is a possible solution to the problem. With your blessing I would like to ride into Grover and put the proposition to both men.'

'Alone?' asked another elder.

'If necessary,' nodded the pastor. 'However, it might be better if one or two of you were to accompany me. Perhaps you should join us, Mr McNally.'

'That'd be one way of makin' sure neither of 'em would agree,' said Brogan. 'It seems that both men are determined to see me dead. Right now is not the time for me to be seen anywhere near the town.'

'Perhaps you are right,' said the pastor. 'Very well, in the absence of any other alternative, I shall ride into Grover tomorrow morning. Do I have any volunteers to accompany me?'

All the elders raised their hands, some plainly more reluctant than others, and it appeared that the pastor was quick to note those who did so willingly and those who did so because they felt they had to. He selected two of the younger-looking members, although Brogan guessed that they were well past their prime. The meeting broke up and all returned to their respective farms, most muttering that they really considered the exercise a waste of time.

'Do you think it will work?' Peter Lloyd asked Brogan when the last of the elders had disappeared.

'Personally, no,' admitted Brogan, 'but I suppose there is a slim chance it might an' since you all refuse to stand your ground an' fight if you have to, I don't see what else you can do.'

'Whilst there is talk there is always hope,' said Peter.

'There'd be even more hope if you was all to band together with your guns,' said Brogan. 'There's more'n enough of you to outshoot 'em if necessary. What about you? Your farm an' the one opposite are the first in line an' the ones most likely to bear the brunt, would you fight on a Sunday to protect your land?'

'The elders have forbidden it,' replied Peter.

'So that's it then?' Brogan laughed sarcastically. 'If they ordered you to shoot yourself or your family, would you do it?'

'They would never make such an order,' replied Peter. 'There are occasions, even allowed for within our faith, when it is in order, nay, even a sacred duty, to take up arms, provided that it is done for the protection of the family or the community.'

'Even on a Sunday?' asked Brogan.

'Even on a Sunday,' confirmed Peter. 'If we were attacked, as has happened in the old days by Indians, it is allowed that arms be taken up to protect oneself.'

'But drivin' a herd of cows through your land on a Sunday don't amount to an attack on the family or the community?'

'Since it is not done with the intention of murdering anyone, no,' replied Peter. 'The fact that it causes damage to crops and perhaps even to property is not reason enough.'

'I give up!' sighed Brogan. 'Maybe I'd be better off just leavin' you to it. At least nobody would be tryin' to kill me.'

'That is your choice,' said Peter. 'I cannot stop you nor would I attempt to.'

'I'll have to think about it,' said Brogan, this time quite serious.

What Brogan actually did was to walk across to the boundary of the farm where it overlooked the slope down towards Grover, just visible in the distance. The land at this point was very rocky with a great many stunted thorn trees and rose quite steeply up the side of the valley. It was quite obvious, to Brogan's mind at least, that it would be impossible to drive cattle across at this point. He slowly walked the boundary of the farm but it was not until he was within about 200 yards of the river that the ground really became flat enough and clear enough to allow cattle through without risk of injury to both cattle and men.

He did not need to cross the river to see that the ground on the opposite side was an almost exact image of the side he was on. In all he estimated that there was at least one and half miles of terrain which was hostile towards the large-scale movement of cattle. That left about half a mile in the centre of the valley along which it was feasible to drive the cattle, and of that only about half was ideal, the strip either side of the river, added to which, 100 yards below the farm boundaries, the river suddenly dropped in a series of rapids, so any cattle approaching would have to be funnelled through narrow gaps one side of the river or the other.

He eventually found himself down by the river which, although about twenty yards wide, was no

more than two feet deep at any point and as such
would present no problem as far as the cattle were
concerned. The one thing he did note was that the
land either side of the river was obviously subject to
flooding from time to time and was apparently not
used for growing crops but as pasture for the few
animals the farmers had. From what he had learned
from the pastor and the elders, this was not necessarily the case further up the valley. Since it was still
about an hour and a half to sundown, he decided to
follow the river upstream for a while.

'Have you reconsidered your involvement?' asked
Peter Lloyd, as he and Brogan sat out on the porch
after the evening meal. 'I saw you walking the river
and you appeared to be deep in thought.'

'I was tryin' to work out ways to stop them cows,'
sighed Brogan. 'It would be easy if you were all to
fight, but since it seems that ain't likely, I was also
lookin' at ways of controllin' just where they went. I
don't know about further up the valley, but at this
end I don't reckon it'd be too difficult an' it won't
cause that much damage. None of you at this end
seem to have much in the way of crops planted down
there.'

'Because of the flooding,' said Peter, confirming
Brogan's suspicions. 'Beyond the lake they do not get
flooding and have therefore both cultivated and
built closer to the river and the lake. However, I do
not believe there would be much difficulty even up
there. The land either side of the river beyond the
lake rises quite steeply, which is where some of us
have sheep. There is little else to be done with it. The

cattle could easily be driven around the lake avoiding the farms and the main fields.'

'You've been thinkin' about it, haven't you?' grinned Brogan. 'I guess that's a step in the right direction.'

'I see little alternative,' smiled Peter. 'With or without our agreement, both Mr Feldmann and Mr Stockwell will drive their cattle through so it is up to us to ensure that they are driven along a path which causes the least damage.'

'That'd mean workin' on a Sunday,' Brogan pointed out. 'It might also mean usin' your guns to frighten the cows into goin' the way you want 'em to go. Ain't that against your religion?'

'I am not certain,' said Peter. 'I would have to consult the pastor and get the agreement of the elders.'

'I reckon some of you should start thinkin' for yourselves once in a while,' said Brogan, sarcastically. 'I reckon you have to get permission from the elders if you want to fart.'

'I do not approve of your choice of words, Brogan,' Peter said with a smile. 'However I am fully aware of what you mean. You may not approve of our way of life, but I do not ask you for your approval. We live the way we do because that is what we believe in. We do not expect others to believe as we do but we would like them to respect our beliefs. Unfortunately this is not always the case. I also believe the Good Lord will help us in our hour of need.'

'Your pastor seems to think that your God is usin' me to help,' Brogan grinned. 'Well He sure ain't asked me if I want to, yet.'

'He will!' said Peter in all seriousness. 'He will!'

Brogan thought about arguing the point but realized that he would probably lose and thought for a moment. 'Have you any dynamite?' he asked.

'Dynamite?' repeated Peter with obvious surprise. 'What on earth do you want dynamite for?'

'I just had this sudden message,' Brogan said, grinning knowingly. 'Maybe this Lord of yours is tryin' to get through to me. . . .' Peter appeared quite serious, apparently believing that Brogan, too, was serious. 'Anyhow, I got this message that I needed some dynamite. Most farmers I know have some. Have you?'

'I do have about five sticks,' nodded Peter. 'It has been a long time since I have even looked at it so I have no idea what condition it is in.'

'That ain't important as long as it blows up when it's supposed to,' said Brogan. 'How about the others?'

'Probably most have some,' nodded Peter. 'It is used occasionally for clearing tree stumps or rock.'

'I don't really have any idea what I'm goin' to do with it, but in the past I've found it pretty useful stuff,' said Brogan. 'Do you think your people will part with a few sticks apiece?'

'I see no reason why not,' said Peter. 'If you like I shall visit the nearer farms in the morning. How much do you think you'll need?'

'The more the better,' Brogan grinned. 'I'd say a couple of dozen sticks ought to be enough.'

'Well, you can certainly have all I have,' said Peter. 'I've even got some fuse somewhere, I'll look it out.'

'You can ask if the others have any fuse as well,' said Brogan.

'There is just one thing I must insist on,' said Peter, 'and I know the others will feel exactly the same. That is that you must not use the dynamite to kill anyone. I think I see what you might use it for, diverting the cattle or even blocking their way through, but I know I speak for the community when I say it must not be used to deliberately kill anyone.'

'Agreed,' said Brogan. 'Mind you, there ain't much I can do about it if someone gets in the way, especially after they've been warned.'

'Providing they are given due warning, that is all I ask,' replied Peter.

Brogan was surprised to see the pastor and the two elders who were accompanying him to Grover call at the Lloyds' farm very shortly after sunrise, but he was quite pleased to see them since he wanted to put his idea about the dynamite to the pastor. He had expected them to embrace the idea but they seemed very doubtful.

'And who is to apply the match to the fuses?' asked the pastor.

'I would've thought that was somethin' you could all take a hand in,' said Brogan. 'Two or three explosions spread across the path of the cows would be far more effective than a solitary one here an' there.'

'Have you considered the implication of what you propose?' asked the pastor.

'I've thought about what might happen if you do nothin',' said Brogan.

'As have we all,' sighed the pastor. 'I have been giving the whole matter some careful consideration but unfortunately I have not, as yet, reached a conclusion which would satisfy both our aims and our beliefs.'

'I don't see no conflict,' said Brogan. 'You either

stand up for yourselves or you get trampled into the dirt, an' I don't just mean by the cows. You back off and you've lost for ever.'

'You may well be right,' said the pastor. 'However; our beliefs are paramount and in no way must the Lord's Day be compromised.'

'Peter did tell me that there are circumstances, even on a Sunday, when it is permissible or even considered obligatory, to fight, such as when you are protecting yourselves or the community.'

'That is true,' nodded the pastor, 'but I have no doubt that he also told you that it is only permissible if the intent of the aggressor is to commit murder.'

'Yeh,' sighed Brogan. 'He told me. He also said that since it is plainly not the intention of Stockwell to murder anyone – except maybe me – there is nothing you can or will do.'

'I can assure you, Mr McNally,' smiled the pastor, 'that should anyone make a deliberate attempt upon your life, there is nobody in the community who would not help you, even to the extent of using his gun.'

'On a Sunday?' asked Brogan, sarcastically. 'I didn't think you would even carry a gun on a Sunday.'

'Even on a Sunday,' said the pastor. 'However, it would appear that you are not grasping the point I am attempting to make. On any other day I would welcome what you suggest and there would be no shortage of volunteers to help you, but in this case it would be the same as taking up arms on a Sunday and, apart from the circumstances you have mentioned, it cannot be allowed.'

'So I might as well forget the whole idea,' Brogan

said with a resigned shrug. 'I don't see why I should worry if you don't. It ain't as if this is my land, my livelihood or my children's future. I might as well ride out here an' now. I sure don't want to help someone who don't want to be helped.'

'That is a decision only you can make,' said the pastor. 'But let me assure you that we would be more than grateful for any help you may care to give. The only point I would make is that you are not bound by our rules concerning either work or the carrying of arms on a Sunday. We cannot and will not dictate to you what you may do on the Lord's Day – although there would be far less conflict in the world if others believed as we do. If you should choose to use this dynamite nobody will attempt to stop you.'

Brogan laughed. 'It's rather like havin' a dog, ain't it?' he said. 'You've all got dogs an' there's nothin' you can do to stop it killin' rats on a Sunday except maybe chain it up, an' even then you can't stop it barkin'. I reckon all of you are bein' plain hypocritical. You ain't prepared to act yourself but you would be quite happy for someone else to do your dirty work for you. No, sir, I'm always ready to help anyone in trouble but I ain't prepared to be used just to satisfy anyone's conscience. I expect co-operation from anyone I'm tryin' to help, even on a Sunday.'

'And co-operation you shall receive,' said the pastor, completely unmoved by Brogan's outburst. 'Do not expect any of us to bear arms against our fellow men, that is all. Now, we must continue on our way. Hopefully, with God's help, there will be no need for anyone to do anything on Sunday. It could be that Mr Stockwell will see the light and agree to delay his cattle drive.'

'Just so's you can start shootin' at him on a Monday an' be able to live with your consciences by not havin' to make a decision on a Sunday,' sneered Brogan. 'I ask you, do you really expect any man not to do somethin' one day just 'cos it don't suit you?'

'We can but hope that he sees reason and does not attempt to move his cattle through the pass at all,' retorted the pastor. 'Perhaps he will even agree to the suggestion of a charge of twenty-five cents a head for the privilege.'

'Do you believe in fairies?' Brogan sneered again. The three elders looked at him questioningly. 'I reckon you must do. You seem to be living in some child's make-believe world.'

'You are, of course, entitled to your opinions,' replied the pastor. 'We shall report to you when we return from Grover, when it is possible, depending upon what the response is, that we shall reassess the situation. Come, Brothers. we have much work to do.'

'Work to avoid, you mean!' Brogan muttered. There was no response from the three and they drove off towards the main trail leaving Brogan seriously considering his position.

'Do not judge us too harshly,' said Peter coming up behind him. 'You must realize that it is just as difficult for us to compromise our beliefs as it is for you to accept our reasons. However, I have the feeling that we shall not be as passive as you might think. I do not know what will happen, but I do have the feeling that the community will not simply sit back and allow it to happen. I do not believe that any of us will take up arms, but I do not believe we will simply stand and watch. Now, do you still require that dynamite?'

'What the hell!' sighed Brogan. 'OK, I guess so. I owe you one for savin' my life. I reckon I'm in it right up to my neck now. Sure, go get all the dynamite you can lay your hands on. While you're doin' that I'll go take a look at the land again an' see if I can figure out a way to stop 'em.'

SEVEN

The arrival of the pastor and the two elders in Grover attracted a fair amount of attention even though it was not unusual for any of the farmers to be seen in the town. Usually they came to sell their produce – which was normally quite eagerly sought after by the townsfolk – and to purchase goods from the stores. The storekeepers liked having the farmers as customers since they always paid in cash, in full and did not try to haggle. This time, however, almost everyone knew that this particular visit was tied up with the impending cattle drives and while a few sympathized with the farmers, most were, at best, completely indifferent to their problem. Their first call was to the sheriff's office.

'We have come to talk to Mr Stockwell and Mr Feldmann,' said the pastor as the sheriff met them outside his office. 'Preferably to Mr Stockwell first.'

'He ain't here right now,' grunted the sheriff, 'but I hear tell he's due in any time now. McGinty's Bar is the best place to wait for him.'

The pastor smiled and shook his head. 'You must know that we are not in the habit of frequenting such places, Sheriff. With your permission we shall wait for him outside your office.'

'I can't stop you waitin' where you've a mind to,' said Gorman. 'If you don't mind me askin', what do you want with Stockwell?'

'Just to talk,' said one of the elders. 'We have a lot to talk about.'

'You might have,' smiled Gorman, 'but I don't reckon he'll feel the same.'

'You know about the cattle drive planned for Sunday?' asked the other elder.

'Ask me who don't,' nodded Gorman. 'If that's what you want to talk to him about I reckon you're wastin' your time. Him an' Feldmann have made their minds up, they're takin' their herds through Bullfrog Pass.'

'And I take it there is nothing you either can or will do to prevent them,' said the pastor. 'Surely there is some law about trespass? On the way here I see large signs declaring that anyone found on either Mr Stockwell's or Mr Feldmann's land is liable to be shot.'

'They ain't worth the wood they is painted on,' laughed Gorman. 'There ain't no law sayin' they can't put up such signs, but as for shootin' anyone that's a different matter. Anyone who did anythin' like that would find themselves in jail on a charge of murder in no time. They're just put there to scare folk. Anyhow, it'd be a mite difficult to prove trespass if they do go through Bullfrog Pass. There's a right of way straight up through the pass, you ought to know that.'

'Agreed,' nodded the pastor, 'but it is no more than a narrow trail, at the widest perhaps twenty feet and at the narrowest no more than ten feet, hardly wide enough to accommodate two thousand head of cattle all at once.'

'I know that, you know that an' both Feldmann an' Stockwell know it,' said Gorman. 'The trouble is the cows don't know it an' it seems that the lawyers don't know it either. They've been cleared on that score. There is no law to prevent any man drivin' whatever he likes along that trail.'

'But two thousand head,' protested one of the elders. 'There is no way that the fencing, where there is fencing, could contain that number; they would simply break it down.'

'That's one of them things,' said Gorman. 'The only thing you could do is to sue for damages in court. The point is that as far as I'm concerned they do have a legal right to use that trail, even with a herd of cattle.'

'Then it seems that we are left with little alternative but to try and appeal to Mr Stockwell's better nature,' said the pastor.

'Better nature!' laughed the sheriff. 'Believe me, neither of them have a better nature unless it has dollar signs all over it.'

'You do know that there have been two attempts on Mr McNally's life?' said the pastor, The sheriff nodded. 'Surely it must be obvious that either Mr Stockwell or Mr Feldmann are behind them, perhaps even both.'

'Obvious?' said Gorman, smiling sardonically, 'Sure, my gut feelin' might agree with you on that but unfortunately – or fortunately dependin' how you look at it – the law demands proof an' gut feelin's certainly don't come into that category. Anyhow, it's up to McNally to make a complaint, but since he ain't done that, there's nothin' I can do about it.

'Nor is he likely to,' said the pastor. 'So it would appear that the law is all on the side of Mr Stockwell and Mr Feldmann and that we have no rights at all. Doesn't Mr Stockwell realize that by driving his herd through on a Sunday he is committing a sin in working on the sabbath and that he will certainly be condemned to Hell's fires when he dies?'

'I won't argue with you on whether it's a sin or not,' said Gorman with a broad smile, 'or whether they'll end up in Hell or not. The fact is it ain't against the law of the land and quite frankly I don't think he gives a damn about bein' sent to Hell when his time comes. As far as I know nobody ain't never come back to say what it's like in either place. Maybe you know somethin' the rest of us don't on that score.'

'We have the writings of the Bible,' said one of the elders, solemnly. 'There can be no greater proof.'

'If that's what you choose to believe, that's fine,' said Gorman. 'Anyhow, I don't have the time to argue the ins an' outs of religion an' neither do you. That's Mr Stockwell comin' into town now an' it looks like if you want to talk to him you'll just have to swallow your principles an' follow him into McGinty's Bar.'

A wagon drew up outside the bar, driven by one man and carrying two others, one of whom was Bradley Stockwell. The pastor did call out to attract his attention but the call was either ignored or went unheard. Reluctantly the three elders crossed the street and went into the bar.

Apart from the fact that Bradley Stockwell actually

owned McGinty's Bar – just as Heinrich Feldmann owned the Black Diamond – it was where he conducted almost all his business when he was in town. Sometimes that business would take place in the main saloon and sometimes it would be conducted in an office at the back. When he saw the three elders it was quite obvious that he intended to conduct any business in the saloon, mainly to embarrass them.

'I am honoured,' he said, smiling sarcastically. 'It isn't often I get a visit from the pastor and two of his elders. I take it, gentlemen, that this visit is not a social one since I know that you normally frown on places such as this.'

'Occasionally even we have to come down a little,' nodded the pastor. Stockwell indicated three chairs opposite him and invited them to sit down. 'I believe you know why we are here, Mr Stockwell,' continued the pastor.

'Do I?' smiled Stockwell. 'I'm not certain that I do. No doubt you will enlighten me.'

'Your cattle drive on Sunday,' said the pastor. 'At least we have been informed that you intend driving about two thousand head through our pass on Sunday.'

'Your information is correct,' said Stockwell with a grin. 'But then it wouldn't need a fortune teller to tell you that, it is common knowledge.'

'But Sunday is the Lord's Day!' objected one of the elders. 'It is a sin to work on a Sunday.'

'Says who?' asked Stockwell.

'The Good Book says so,' replied the elder. 'You must know what I say is true. Were you not brought up with Christian beliefs?'

'I was raised with a belief in work,' replied Stockwell. 'Now, if all you've come to do is preach at me, forget it. I go to church every now an' then in the town, which seems to be enough for our minister. Get to the point, what do you want?'

'We want you to take your cattle round the way you usually do,' said the pastor. 'For many years now you have driven them across the McKenzie Plains, why do you now need to go through Bullfrog Pass?'

'I wouldn't've thought you needed me to tell you why,' sneered Stockwell. 'Until this last two years, goin' across the McKenzie Plains was the only way to the railroad. Since they took the new railroad through Banksville it's cut the time needed to drive the herds by a week but to make that savin' we now have to go through Bullfrog Pass. Anyhow, I have it on the best advice from the best lawyers in the state that we are quite within our rights to use the trail through the pass.'

'So we hear,' nodded the other elder. 'That would be fine if the trail could cope with that number of animals all at once, but it can't. There must obviously be a great deal of damage.'

'There isn't that much I can do about it,' laughed Stockwell. 'Of course, my men will try to ensure that the herd keeps to the trail, but unfortunately cows have no sense of right and wrong, they do not differentiate between who owns what land and which is a right of way.'

'So nothing we can say will make you change your mind,' said the pastor. 'Why do you have to make your point on a Sunday? You must know that it offends our beliefs.'

'But it don't offend mine,' said Stockwell. 'I chose

Sunday mainly because I thought that you and your people would do something stupid like try to stop us on any other day and that could have led to someone bein' killed or at least hurt bad and, like you, I don't want anything like that to happen.'

'But I ask you to consider the damage that such a drive will do,' said the pastor. 'At this time of the year the crops are beginning to come through and a herd of cows would destroy everything.'

'Like I said,' said Stockwell, 'there's not a lot I can do about that. My men will be under instruction to keep the herd to the trail wherever possible.'

'But you know that will be impossible,' said the pastor.

'I don't know nothin' of the kind,' grinned Stockwell.

'What about compensation for the damage?' said one of the elders. 'I have heard of cases where the cattle owner has compensated farmers for damage to their crops.'

'I hear tell there's what they call insurance which covers such things,' said Stockwell. 'As a matter of fact I'm thinkin' about takin' out some of that insurance stuff for myself, I've got me a salesman comin' next month. Maybe you should talk to him and see if there's anythin' he can do.'

'I . . . er . . . we were thinking of a somewhat different scheme,' said the pastor. 'We were considering allowing your herds use of a predetermined path through the valley on condition that you pay twenty five cents a head for the privilege.'

Bradley Stockwell suddenly threw back his head and laughed loudly. 'You've been talkin' to Feldmann. He had that idea too an' I have to admit that at first I thought it wasn't half bad, but I've been talkin' to the lawyers an' since they told me that I have right of way along the trail, there isn't any need.'

'We have not been talking to Mr Feldmann,' said the pastor. 'As a matter of fact, the suggestion came from a certain Mr Brogan McNally. You probably know all about him; I believe either you or Mr Feldmann have tried twice to murder him.'

The expression on Bradley Stockwell's face suddenly changed into a snarl and he sat upright. 'I might have known his interfering was in this somewhere. For a saddletramp that man sure sticks his nose into a lot of business that isn't his. As for trying to murder him, I wouldn't go round making accusations like that if I were you. Now, since you brought the subject of this McNally up, I've got a proposition to put to you: I drive my cattle through your valley and I'll even guarantee two hundred and fifty dollars as compensation for damage, but there is one condition and that is that you hand McNally over to me. I don't care if you hand over a dead body, just so long as you hand him over.'

'You are asking us to sell a man's soul for our own selfish desires,' said the pastor. 'I think you must know the answer to that proposition, but before I say definitely, pray tell us why you are so intent on murdering this man?'

'I never said nothing about murder,' said Stockwell. 'That's against the law. If he has an accident either before you hand him over or maybe afterwards, that would be his misfortune. The point is that neither I nor Heinrich Feldmann intend to allow any saddletramp to tell us what we can or cannot do and nor do we intend to stand by while he attempts to organize a raggle-taggle community like yours into standing in defiance. Neither of the attempts on his life was anything to do with me. It was an attempt by Heinrich Feldmann in the first instance to lay the blame on me by making it look like my men, Semple and Grayson, wanted to kill him because he made them look small in this very bar. What Feldmann didn't know was that they were both in jail at the time, so it backfired on him.'

'Whatever the reason,' said the pastor, 'the price you ask is too high. We thank you for listening to us, Mr Stockwell, and we are sorry that we cannot make you change your mind. It now remains to be seen just how successful your drive on Sunday will be. I shall not wish you luck since we hope that you fail. However, please remember that even we realize when we need to change our attitudes in some way and we are still prepared to offer both your and Mr Feldmann's cattle unrestricted access along a prede-termined route on payment of twenty-five cents a head. That way we all benefit, you by getting your animals to market that much quicker and therefore in better condition and we at least get adequate compensation for the damage done to our crops.'

'And you can all go to hell!' snarled Stockwell. 'No rancher worth his salt ever kow-tows to a dirt farmer.'

'As you wish,' said the pastor. 'Come, Brothers, we appear to have overstayed our welcome. Good day to you, Mr Stockwell, may the Lord forgive you for what you intend doing.'

'I'd say it was you who needed help from Him,' said Stockwell. 'I'll be startin' them cows at first light on Sunday an' when they start movin' you're goin' to need all the help you can get. Cows can't read notices an' they don't care about treading someone into the ground. Good day to you all.' He slammed his fist down on the table, stood up and stormed through to the office at the back. The three elders left the saloon wondering if they had achieved anything at all.

'Don't say I didn't warn you,' said Brogan when the pastor told him of their failed mission. 'I ain't surprised he wanted you to hand me over, it sure would've saved him a lot of bother. Anyhow, I ain't been idle while you've been away. Peter got me twenty-eight sticks of dynamite, more'n enough I should think. I've been takin' another look at where they're likely to take the cattle through an' I have a few ideas. I ain't too sure if they'll work or not but then I never do have an' it seems it nearly always does.'

'Spare us the details, Mr McNally,' said the pastor. 'The less we know at this stage the better.'

'On the basis that what you don't know you can't be blamed for, either by your God, or the sheriff,' taunted Brogan. 'I hear tell there's this big bird, stands more'n six feet tall, in some place called Africa an' when it gets scared, it sticks its head in the sand an' pretends it can't be seen since it can't see nothin'. Don't know if there is such a bird or not, personally I don't think so, whoever heard of a six foot tall bird?'

'There is such a bird,' said the pastor with a knowing smile. 'You are quite correct, it does live in Africa, and it does, apparently, bury its head when it is frightened. I take your point, Mr McNally, it must appear to someone like you that we are desperately looking for ways to hide ourselves from the inevitable. Let me assure you that despite all outward apperances, we shall not be found wanting when the time comes.'

'I'm glad to hear it,' said Brogan. 'OK, I won't tell you my idea, I'll keep it as a surprise.'

Whilst the pastor and the elders had been trying to talk to Bradley Stockwell in Grover, Brogan had once again walked the boundaries of the Lloyd farm and the one on the opposite side of the river. He had been armed with the sticks of dynamite, a quantity of fuse and a spade and had buried dynamite at what he considered strategic spots. Of the twenty-eight sticks, he had buried twenty, keeping the remainder back for possible use in case any of the buried sticks failed to explode or the cattle were not deterred.

He had tried to explain to Peter Lloyd just where and why he had buried the dynamite but it was glaringly obvious that he was not interested and, like the pastor, still insistent that all would be well on the day. However, he thanked Brogan for all his efforts and did, reluctantly, agree that it was perhaps as well that there was some other line of defence.

'Other line of defence?' queried Brogan. 'From what I've seen an' heard you ain't got a first one.'

'We have the Lord,' said Peter with a smile. 'I fully appreciate your doubts, Brogan, and I know to people like you we must appear somewhat eccentric, but that is our way.'

'Will this Lord of yours be providin' you with guns and bullets?'

'He will be providing us with a great deal more than that,' said Peter. 'Against His power bullets are but as dried peas blown through a child's peashooter.'

'I think I'll put my faith in a good old piece of lead,' muttered Brogan. 'Anyhow, I've done what I can. We'll see if your Lord can make a bigger bang than a stick of dynamite.'

'Let me assure you, Brogan,' laughed Peter, 'He is capable of making a bang so large that it would shake the whole world.'

'I guess I'll just have to take your word for that,' Brogan mumbled. 'Frankly I think I've been wastin' my time.'

'I do not dismiss your efforts on our behalf,' said Peter. 'Our ways are the ways of the Lord but we are not privy to His thoughts. It is more than possible that your actions are guided by His hand and that your way will be the only way. All I say is that contrary to your opinion, we shall not simply stand and allow our way of life to trampled underfoot.'

'Then just what do you intend doin'?' asked Brogan. 'I think you've all made it pretty damned plain that you won't be usin' any guns.'

'There is a meeting tonight,' said Peter. 'Perhaps you should attend and be enlightened.'

'I don't need no enlightenment,' said Brogan. 'If you don't mind, I'll give it a miss, I ain't into all that prayin' an' stuff.'

'A pity,' smiled Peter. 'About you not being into all that praying and stuff I mean. Perhaps if more people were there would not be so much violence in the world.'

'Maybe so,' agreed Brogan. 'Unfortunately that ain't how the real world is.'

Brogan felt that he had heard enough and

decided to take another walk around the boundaries, this time taking his rifle since he had the idea of shooting at some of the fuses to set them alight, something he had done before with reasonable success, but he needed to establish exactly where to aim at. He could not get out of his mind that the farmers had obviously decided on some course of action or other and, even though he had declined the offer to attend the meeting that evening, he could not help but wonder just what crazy ideas they had cooked up. Eventually, for his own peace of mind, he decided that he would attend.

When he reached the point where he had buried the first stick of dynamite – behind a small boulder – and had checked that it was still in place and he had placed a stone at which to aim, he looked out towards Grover and saw a tell-tale cloud of dust approaching the valley.

At first it was impossible to tell how many men there were, but it was obvious that there were several horses. Eventually it became clear that there were six of them. Automatically he checked his Colt and his Winchester and waited until the riders came closer. He did not recognize any of them but it was plain that they knew who he was as they pulled up a few yards away and for some moments they eyed each other.

'McNally, ain't it?' grated the man who appeared to be the leader. 'Mr Stockwell warned us that you might be around.'

'Then he was right,' replied Brogan. 'I don't reckon he told you what to do if I was though.'

'He didn't say nothin',' confirmed the man. He glanced nervously at the others and licked his lips.

'It's common knowledge that he wants to see you dead, though.'

'And you're the men to do it, are you?' sneered Brogan. 'Go ahead, make a name for yourselves. There's six of you an' there's six bullets in my gun. Maybe I won't be able to kill all of you before you kill me, but which four of you are ready to die first?'

'None of us are gunfighters,' replied the man, hoarsely. 'We're cowhands. It ain't our job to kill nobody. None of us ain't never even shot a man before, let alone killed one an' we ain't about to start now, not even for Mr Stockwell.'

'What you doin' up here then,' laughed Brogan, 'lookin' for strays?'

'We were sent to make sure them farmers warn't puttin' up no barricades,' said one of the others.

'And if they were?' asked Brogan.

'We was to pull 'em down,' said the man.

'Well,' smiled Brogan, 'look about you. I don't see no barricades, do you?'

'Guess not,' replied the man. 'But we was also told to stay up here an' keep an eye on just what you're all doin'.'

'I guess I can't stop you,' said Brogan. 'I hope you don't mind if I stay around an' keep an eye on just what you're doin' as well.'

Although it had been his intention to go to the meeting, the arrival of these men put a different aspect on things. He knew that he had been fortunate in being able to place his explosives before they had arrived but the one thing he was now certain of was that he could not take the risk of them discovering it.

'I guess you got that right,' muttered the leader.

'OK, boys, we'll camp out by them trees over there.'
He indicated a group of thorn trees.

'Just one thing,' said Brogan, 'this here is private
land. You stay well that side of the boundary an' I'll
stay this side an' don't any man get the idea of
crossin' the boundary 'cos it might just be that the
rest of you will have to carry his body back.'

'We hear what you say, McNally,' rasped the leader.
'Don't worry, we don't like this any more'n you do.'

'Then why do it?' asked Brogan.

The man laughed. 'Even we have to eat, McNally,'
he said, 'an' Mr Stockwell pays better'n most.'

'Just remember, keep to your own side,' said
Brogan.

EIGHT

As far as Brogan was concerned, it was obvious that
Bradley Stockwell's men had no intention of doing
anything other than obey the literal meaning of their
orders, which was to keep an eye on whatever the
farmers and Brogan were doing. Since that was
apparently nothing, there was little for them to do
and they spent most of their time sitting around a
fire. It was about three hours after nightfall that
Brogan felt easy enough to return to the farm for the
night, quite sure that they would stay where they
were. The following morning the men were still
among the thorn trees and did not appear to have
moved. Even so, Brogan casually patrolled the
boundary to ensure that none of his dynamite had
been discovered and succeeded in placing markers
at which to aim, without apparently attracting too
much attention.

During the day, Peter Lloyd's two elder sons took
over the task of watching Stockwell's men, but apart
from two visits by a man they identified as the ranch
foreman, nothing happened. Brogan also tried to get
Peter and Mary Lloyd to tell him exactly what the
community had planned for the Sunday, but it

seemed that either they were not prepared to tell him or were under orders not to. He suspected the latter.

Stockwell's men eventually left their post just after midday on Saturday and from a high vantage point Brogan and Peter Lloyd could see the reason. Large numbers of cattle were being brought together in the pastures belonging to Bradley Stockwell and the men were obviously required to help control them. They also saw a long section of boundary fencing being dismantled in readiness for the drive.

'It would appear that they are quite determined to go ahead,' sighed Peter. 'It is a pity, I'm quite certain that given more time we could have agreed.'

'Maybe you should've thought about it before now,' said Brogan. 'It strikes me some of them elders of yours need puttin' out to graze as well. Times change, you need younger men who can adapt.'

'Such a thing has been suggested,' grinned Peter. 'In fact there are rumblings amongst the younger farmers, such as me, that we form our own council.'

Brogan laughed loudly. 'Now if I was a religious man I'd say that kind of talk almost amounts to—' He was plainly struggling for the right word. 'Heredity,' he said eventually. 'That ain't the word I want, but I know it's somethin' like that.'

'Heresy!' laughed Peter. 'That's very true and there are many of the present elders who would certainly look upon such a suggestion as just that. However, there are those amongst us, myself included and, I do believe, our pastor, who realize that as the world changes, so must we.'

'Well right now is not the time to start a revolution,' said Brogan. 'Maybe after this is all over, but just now you all need to stand together.'

'And stand together we shall,' nodded Peter.

Although Brogan was the first person up and about in the Lloyd household, he was not at all surprised to discover, on going outside, that a large number of other farmers were beginning to congregate. He had been very aware of activity since about an hour before dawn. The pastor was also among them and Brogan approached him.

'Maybe someone had better tell me just what's goin' on,' he said. 'I guessed that you had somethin' in mind from what Peter said.'

'We are gathered to make our protest,' smiled the pastor.

'Meanin' what exactly?' asked Brogan. 'It don't look to me like any of you have any guns an' I hope you understand I don't mean no disrespect when I say that guns are the only thing what are goin' to solve the immediate problem, if only to scare the cows.'

The pastor smiled indulgently. 'It is the sabbath, remember,' he said. 'We are not armed nor shall we be. This is the Lord's Day and He shall be on our side. Anyway, I am given to understand that you have taken some precautions.'

'I guess you could say that,' sighed Brogan. 'Just tell your people to stay well out of the way when them cows start movin' 'cos there's likely to be some loud bangs an' some dirt flyin' about.'

'They have already been warned,' said the pastor.

'Well I'm goin' up on that big rock up there.' He pointed at the large rock from where they had

witnessed the gathering of the cattle the day before.
'I'll yell when they start movin' 'em out.'

'And I shall organize my people,' said the pastor.
Brogan could not help but feel very uneasy at that
suggestion.

'Which means what?' he asked again.

'You will see,' beamed the pastor.

'That's just what I'm afraid of,' Brogan grumbled,
knowing that he was not going to get any further
information from anyone and it worried him even
further that even small children seemed to be
involved and that most people were wandering about
with huge grins.

He was joined on the rock by Peter Lloyd and
although Brogan tried to get further information
out of him, it seemed that even at this stage Peter was
not prepared to tell him. They stood on the rock,
Brogan using an ancient spyglass that he always
carried in his saddle-bag, and watched as the men
below gathered the cows together. Brogan identified
Bradley Stockwell, but he appeared to be leaving
most of the organizing to his foreman. About an
hour after sunrise the herd was suddenly urged
forward.

'They're comin'!' Brogan called to the pastor. 'It'll
probably take 'em about half an hour to reach here.'

'We shall be ready!' shouted the pastor.

'Just what the hell does he mean by that?' Brogan
demanded of Peter Lloyd. 'What the hell is goin' on?
I need to know, I don't want anyone gettin' hurt by
the explosions.'

'I don't think you do really want to know,' laughed
Peter. 'If you don't mind, I shall join the others now.'

'And maybe I should just get on my old horse an'

get the hell out of here,' grumbled Brogan. 'I have this feelin' that I ain't goin' to like what I see.'

'You still have time,' replied Peter. 'I do not think that anyone would blame you if you did.'

'An' I wouldn't give a damn if you all blamed me or not,' said Brogan.

'There's a whole load of folk up there,' said the foreman to Bradley Stockwell as the herd started moving. 'Slim Watkins has this spyglass an' he says they just seem to be standin' around waitin'.'

'I suppose it's not every day that they have two thousand head of cattle tramplin' through their farms,' said Stockwell. 'Let them look, I guess there's no law against that.'

'Slim also says that he thinks this McNally feller is up on a big rock,' said the foreman. 'He seems to be directin' them in some way.'

'Are the farmers armed?' asked Stockwell.

The foreman called to the man with the spyglass and repeated the question. 'He says it don't look like it,' he said eventually.

'I heard him,' said Stockwell. 'I didn't think they would be. I'm even surprised that they've gathered to watch, I'd've thought they would have been in their church prayin' for a miracle. I don't know what McNally thinks he's doing, but when this is over, I want that man's hide stretched across a firescreen in my livin'-room just so's he can roast.'

'If he should happen to get in the way of a few cows an' get himself trampled to death, will that do?' asked the foreman.

'I guess so,' nodded Stockwell. 'I would have prefered to have killed him myself, but I suppose it would

look better as far as the law is concerned. Tell the
men there's a bonus for the one who happens to
cause McNally to have an accident.'

'Yes, sir!' grinned the foreman who then rode off
to tell the others.

'Get them dogies moving faster!' yelled Stockwell.

'They're drivin' 'em faster,' said Brogan as he ran
down the slope to the pastor. 'Get your people out of
the way. If you don't intend puttin' up a fight, I guess
I'll have to.' He looked in horror as the farmers and
their families suddenly began spreading themselves
across the path of the cattle. 'What the hell do they
think they're doin'?' he yelled at the pastor. 'They'll
all get 'emselves killed.'

'If that is the Lord's will, then so be it,' smiled the
pastor. 'I am afraid that you will have to delay your
explosions, Mr McNally.' He too went to join the line
of people now stretching across the valley, some even
standing in the river and all clutching their Bibles.

'Christ!' spat Brogan loudly, although it was appar-
ent that he was now talking to himself. 'I might've
known they'd do somethin' stupid like this. Cows
don't read no Bible,' he called out to those closest.
'As far as they're concerned they'll just trample you
all underfoot an' think nothin' of it.' The only
responses were a few smiles and understanding nods.
Suddenly the pastor started singing a hymn, the
sound gradually rising as it was picked up along the
line.

'What the hell do they think they're doin'?' yelled
Bradley Stockwell above the sound of thousands of
hooves pounding the ground. 'They're all standin' in

line, right in the path of the cattle. They'll all be killed.'

'They're about a hundred an' fifty yards ahead,' said the foreman. 'What do we do, Mr Stockwell, turn the herd or drive straight through?'

'Keep on moving!' ordered Stockwell. 'If they want to commit suicide that's up to them. They won't though, you watch, they'll soon start running.'

'Even if they do.' the foreman pointed out, 'there's some of 'em just ain't goin' to make it in time.'

'That's their tough shit!' screamed Stockwell. 'Get them moving faster.'

'They ain't goin' to get out of the way!' shouted the foreman. 'Christ, Mr Stockwell, there's women with babes in arms an' small children. We can't just let the cattle run 'em down.'

'You heard!' shouted Stockwell, his eyes glaring hatred. 'I ain't about to let a bunch of dirt farmers stand in my way.'

'Sorry, Mr Stockwell,' shouted the foreman, 'I can't just stand by an' let you do this an' it looks like the men can't either look, they're already startin' to turn the herd.'

'You'll all do what I tell you,' screamed Stockwell. 'If you don't, you're all fired. Do you understand me? You're all fired!'

However, his words fell upon deaf ears as all the men were now racing around the front of the herd trying to turn them. For a few moments it looked as though they were fighting a losing battle as, by that time the animals had developed quite a speed. Gunshots were suddenly heard as the men tried to frighten the cows into turning but at first this seemed only to make the cows surge forward faster.

Brogan looked on in a mixture of disbelief and horror as the farmers and their families stood their ground, still clutching their Bibles and still singing. The cows were now no more than fifty yards away and still surging forward and it was all Brogan could do to watch – watch the inevitable, he thought. Suddenly four riders succeeded in turning the leading cows and the remainder simply followed. Although the herd came to within about twenty-five yards of the farmers and a couple of them actually broke through the line, there did not appear to be any injuries.

Once the herd was turned, Brogan breathed more easily, the immediate danger had passed and the herd eventually came to halt, contained by the ranch hands. Bradley Stockwell was plainly incensed and rode towards the line of farmers, waving his hands and shouting. The pastor eventually stepped forward to meet him.

'Are you all crazy or somethin'!' he shouted at the pastor. 'You could've got quite a few of your people killed.'

'If that is the Lord's will, then we are prepared to die,' replied the pastor.

'I always knew you were crazy,' snarled Stockwell. 'OK, you've made your point, but you can't stand in our way forever. I can assure you that the next time the herd won't be turned.'

'And when is the next time to be?' asked the pastor.

'Pretty damned soon!' grated Stockwell. 'You just make sure your people get out of the way.'

'We shall see,' said the pastor.

Stockwell rode back to his men and there followed

a heated argument with his foreman and several of
the men, after which the cattle were herded back
almost to where they had started. Brogan saw
Stockwell ride off and for another hour nothing
happened.

'He's comin' back,' Brogan called from his vantage
point. 'This time he's got six other men with him an'
if I'm right, these men won't try to turn the cows
once they've started movin'. They're his six hired
guns an' they don't give a damn about anyone bein'
killed.'

'What about the other men?' panted Peter Lloyd,
as he joined Brogan.

'I think Stockwell's sendin' 'em away,' said Brogan.
'It sure looks like it. I'd say the hired guns are takin'
over. You've got to persuade that pastor of yours that
this time the same tactics just ain't goin' to work.'

'I think you're right,' said Peter. 'I must admit that
most of the younger farmers did not particularly like
the idea of standing in line and I think that this time
the elders will be ignored. I'll go and explain what is
happening.' He ran off and found the pastor and
most of the elders. After a few obviously heated
exchanges, the line of people was ordered back.
Brogan watched for a few moments as Bradley
Stockwell organized his new men and then he ran
down the hill to join the farmers.

'They're comin',' he panted. 'This time don't try
nothin' as stupid as before.'

'It worked once,' said one of the elders, 'it will
work again.'

'Not with men like Arnie Semple an' Phil Grayson
runnin' the show,' said Brogan. 'They're killers an''

they don't much care just who they kill nor how they kill.'

'Unfortunately, Brothers,' said the pastor, 'I do believe that on this occasion we must listen to Mr McNally. We have made our point very forcibly and you should all be proud of yourselves, but now it is Mr McNally's turn to hold them off.'

'Then get your folk further back,' said Brogan. 'There's liable to be some rock flyin' about.'

The farmers pulled back well away from the likely route of the cattle and Brogan checked his rifle and then the nearest sticks of dynamite, the ones he would use a cheroot to light the fuses with. He lit his cheroot, made certain that it was burning well and then watched as the herd came nearer.

This time they were being driven even faster and Bradley Stockwell could be seen urging the animals forward. Brogan thought that he was laughing, probably believing that the farmers had backed down. When the animals were about 100 yards away, Brogan knelt down, drew on his cheroot and applied it to the first fuse before running to the second and then on to the others. In all, five fuses were lit and, if Brogan had calculated the length of each fuse correctly, all five should explode at the same time. By that time the cattle were no more than seventy-five yards away and Brogan stood on top of a small mound and took aim at a stick of dyna-mite buried closer to the charging animals but between them and the river and some distance from the fuses he had lit.

His shot proved deadly accurate as it struck home – a very short fuse – and almost immediately there was a loud explosion, a shower of rock and dirt and terrified cows swerved, forcing all the others to turn slightly but not enough. Brogan found himself cursing as the fuses he had lit appeared to take much longer to detonate the dynamite than he had expected. Suddenly, as the leading cows were no more than thirty yards away, there were several, almost simultaneous explosions, quickly followed by at least two others across the path of the herd.

Brogan felt a broad grin cross his face as the animals once again turned, even though they were being urged forward by shouting and shooting. However, the now completely terrified beasts had decided that they were going home and nothing was going to stop them. A loud cheer followed the sight of the cattle rapidly heading back to safer ground and another hearty cheer greeted Brogan as he stepped up towards the pastor and the elders.

'We have won!' beamed the pastor. 'Between us, Mr McNally, we have won.'

'If you say so,' said Brogan, slightly annoyed that the pastor also claimed a stake in the success. 'Maybe they've just been slowed down a bit. I wouldn't celebrate too soon if I was you.'

'They must surely realize that we mean business,' said one of the elders. 'That even on the sabbath we can thwart them.'

'If you don't mind me sayin' so,' grunted Brogan, 'if you had had your way you'd all have stood in line again only that time you would've been killed for certain. I think I can rightly claim that it was me who sent 'em packin' the second time, none of you had anythin' to do with it.'

'The Good Lord was with us,' declared another elder.

Brogan rounded on the man with a ferocity which surprised everybody. 'The Good Lord had nothin' at all to do with it,' he rasped. 'It was thanks to me an' some dynamite. If I hadn't been around some of you would be pickin' dead bodies out of the mud now, so don't give me no shit about this Good Lord of yours bein' on your side an' havin' a hand in it.'

'It was the will of God however it was achieved,' interrupted the pastor. 'The fact that you may not agree with our interpretation of events does not alter a thing. You can claim – and quite rightly from your viewpoint – that it was you who succeeded, while we can argue with equal feeling that it was the Good Lord who guided you, that it was He who arranged for you to come to us, whatever the circumstances, that it was His way of ensuring our safety and our way of life.'

Brogan threw up his arms and laughed loudly. 'OK, OK, I give in! I guess nobody can argue against that kind of logic. It's like a gamblin' man I once knew who won a lot of money usin' two coins, one with two heads an' one with two tails. He got folk to bet either heads or tails, worked out in his head which side most money was on, slipped whichever coin he wanted into his hand so no matter which side it came down most folk lost an' he always won.'

For some time they watched the cattle being rounded up and driven back. It was noticeable that the original hands were soon back patrolling the length of boundary where the fencing had been removed and that Stockwell and his hired guns were riding back towards Grover. Brogan guessed that they had probably seen the last of any attempt to drive the cattle through that day.

*

'Got the better of you, did they?' said Heinrich Feldmann when he met Bradley Stockwell in the back office of McGinty's Bar. 'I'm not gloating, in fact I was all behind you. If you had succeeded, my drive would have been that much easier. What happened?'

'I'm surprised you don't already know,' grunted Stockwell. 'One thing is for certain, if that saddle-bum McNally hadn't been there there I wouldn't be back here now, we'd've been almost through the pass by now.'

'You allowed one man to stop you taking two thousand head of cattle through?' said Feldmann. 'The story is that the farmers all lined up across the valley and just stood there so you had to turn the herd.'

'Yeh, that's what happened the first time,' admitted Stockwell. 'I don't think McNally had anythin' to do with that though, I can't see that kind of thing being his way. The second time was definitely all down to him though, he planted dynamite an' spooked the cows into turning. I reckon he's got the whole of that end of the pass seeded with dynamite. If we had gone through again we'd probably have lost a whole lot of animals. I couldn't take the risk.'

'So now what?' asked Feldmann. 'We have to go through Bullfrog Pass.'

The office door opened and the bartender peered round almost apologetically. 'There's some of the farmers here to talk to you, Mr Stockwell,' he said.

'So now it seems we talk,' sighed Stockwell. 'OK, show them in.'

*

About two hours after all the excitement had subsided and most of the farmers had wandered back to their farms, Peter Lloyd found Brogan in the process of grooming his horse.

'We have decided that we have to go into Grover and talk to both Mr Stockwell and Mr Feldmann,' he said. 'We are quite certain that any difficulties can be resolved.'

'An' just who is "we"?' asked Brogan.

'The younger farmers I was telling you about,' smiled Peter. 'There was a fairly quick meeting of the entire community at which I put forward the idea of a younger committee. I must admit that even I was surprised when the vote in our favour was more than three to one and it included our pastor, but I expected that. It now seems that you are looking at the new leader of the committee.'

'I don't suppose some of the elders liked that very much,' smiled Brogan.

'There were one or two who objected strongly,' said Peter. 'They tried to claim that it was God's will that the elders were made up of the older members. However, there were some who agreed that it was time for change and that the best people to implement change were the younger generation.'

'Well I wish you the best of luck with Feldmann an' Stockwell,' said Brogan. I won't leave just yet, I'll hang about to see what happens but I have the feelin' that you will sort things out. Anyhow, I reckon I'd better go dig up the dynamite I didn't use, I'd hate for some kid to find it an' do somethin' stupid like blow themselves up.'

'A wise precaution,' nodded Peter. 'Like you, I believe that we shall come to an agreement which is favourable to all. I think almost everyone realizes that the cattle will have to come through the pass so we might as well live with the best deal we can get.'

While Peter Lloyd and three other members of the new council rode off to Grover, Brogan went to retrieve the dynamite.

NINE

'What's this?' asked Bradley Stockwell looking very surprised when the three farmers entered the room. 'I thought only what you call the elders were allowed to talk to folk like me.'

'There have been some changes,' said Peter Lloyd. 'In a way I suppose that we have to thank you for what you tried to do, at least it made the Council of Elders listen to us younger ones. The result is you are now talking to three members of the new council. Allow me to introduce my fellow members. . . .' He indicated the two men who were on his right. 'Samuel Drummond and Paul Graham. My name is Peter Lloyd. I own the first farm in the pass.'

'You're the feller who's been looking after that saddlebum, McNally, aren't you?' said Feldmann.

'My wife and I helped nurse Mr McNally back to health,' nodded Peter. 'We were doing nothing other than our Christian duty.'

'Maybe you should have let him die,' grunted Stockwell, 'It might have saved us all a whole heap of trouble.'

'It might have saved you a lot of bother,' said Peter. 'We owe Mr McNally a great debt. It is most unlikely

that without his help we would be here now
discussing the problem.'

'That's just what I mean about trouble,' muttered
Stockwell, 'OK, so you're the ones in charge up there
now. What can I do for you? I don't suppose for one
moment that this is a social visit just to let me know
you're in charge, especially after what happened this
morning.'

'I believe that we made our point this morning,'
said Peter. 'You are quite right, this is not a social
visit, this is business. The point is – and we are
pleased that we have managed to get both of you
together, since it means that we don't have to explain
twice – that we would like to discuss the problem
and, hopefully, come to some agreement which
would satisfy all parties.'

Stockwell glanced at Feldmann and then nodded.
'Talk!' he said. 'We're both listening, but before you
start, do I detect McNally's finger in this somewhere?'

'Mr McNally knows nothing other than we were
coming to speak to you, but he is in full agreement
with us,' assured Peter. 'We are, of course, most grateful to Mr McNally for all that he has done for us, but
he is a drifter and will be moving on shortly.'

'How soon?' demanded Feldmann.

'I suspect probably tomorrow,' said Peter. 'Is it
important?'

'Not really, I just wanted to know when he's likely
to be out of my hair.' muttered Feldmann. 'OK,
we're both listening, talk away.'

'Well it is obvious that both of you are quite determined to take your cattle through Bullfrog Pass,' said
Peter. 'We also understand why it is so important to

you that you do so, since we also use the railroad at Banksville to transport much of our produce. On the other hand, we have lived and farmed in the pass for more than forty years now, far longer than either of you have been here and ten years before the first houses were built in what is now Grover, so we do have certain prior rights and claims.'

'I guess we can't argue with that,' nodded Stockwell, 'and I have to admit that before they put the railroad through Banksville there was no need to bother about Bullfrog Pass.'

'It is almost a pity that they built that railroad,' said Samuel Drummond. 'It is most unfortunate that a decision taken in another part of the country can have such an effect on previously harmonious communities. The point is, Mr Stockwell, we are not seeking confrontation with anyone and would like to live together harmoniously once more. To that end, are you prepared to talk seriously about reaching an agreement?'

Bradley Stockwell once again looked at Heinrich Feldmann and both men nodded. 'I guess so,' sighed Stockwell, 'but that idea of that pastor of yours about charging twenty-five cents a head is just not on.'

This time the three farmers looked at each other. 'That is a pity, Mr Stockwell,' said Paul Graham, 'because charging a levy is the cornerstone of our proposal. . . .'

'Well how'd it go?' asked Brogan when Peter Lloyd returned later that day. The look on his face told him that something had been achieved.

'We managed to reach an agreement!' beamed Peter. 'It was hard and we possibly did not get as much as we might have hoped, but I believe that what has been agreed means that nobody will lose out.'

'I knew you could do it!' grinned Mary, slipping her arms around her husband's neck in a rare show of affection. 'How much did you get?'

'Fifteen cents a head,' said Peter. 'Both Mr Stockwell and Mr Feldmann started off by refusing to pay anything and we began by refusing to accept less than twenty-five cents a head. Eventually we arrived at the figure of fifteen cents. Of course, the agreement has to be sanctioned by the whole council – and I shall bring in the old elders on that – but I do not believe there will be much strong resistance, especially now that most folk realize there just is not any alternative.'

'Well if you're satisfied with that much, I guess that's all that matters,' said Brogan. 'Are you quite certain that they will honour it?'

'It has been agreed that we all meet again in the morning when we shall go to a lawyer and have a legal agreement drawn up and signed,' said Peter. 'I foresee no problems from now on, which means that you are free to leave whenever you want to, Brogan.'

'I didn't know I wasn't free,' said Brogan.

'No, but you know what I mean,' said Peter. 'I must thank you for everything you have done for us.'

'I didn't do that much,' said Brogan.

'Apart from being on hand to do something which we felt we could not do on a Sunday,' said Peter, 'you have been instrumental in bringing about much needed change to our community and we, the younger generation, thank you for that.'

'It had to come,' said Brogan, feeling slightly

smug. 'If it hadn't been me it'd have been sure to have been someone or somethin' else.'

'Perhaps so,' agreed Peter. 'However it happened, it was plainly the will of the Lord.'

'Don't start that argument again,' grunted Brogan. 'There ain't no arguin' against that kind of logic.'

In a rare show of unity, Bradley Stockwell and Heinrich Feldmann gathered their hired guns together in the Black Diamond, Stockwell's men on one side and Feldmann's on the other, each eyeing the other side warily.

'As you all must know by now,' said Feldmann, 'certain things happened when Mr Stockwell tried to drive his herd through Bullfrog Pass and we have been forced to make an agreement with the farmers as a result. Perhaps it is for the better, who knows, but it is not this agreement that we want to talk to you about, that is a matter between the farmers, ourselves and the lawyer. You must all also be aware that just one man was instrumental in bringing this agreement about, a certain Mr Brogan McNally. . . .' He looked at Jess Smith and Gus Tranter and smiled. 'A couple of you have greater cause to remember him than most,' he continued, 'and two of you –' he looked at Arnie Semple and Phil Grayson – 'have no cause to thank him for anything. As far as I know the rest of you have not had to face up to him.'

'The point is,' said Stockwell, 'if it hadn't been for McNally this agreement would have been totally unnecessary. Now you are all men who are used to earning your living by your guns and we are going to

give you the opportunity to earn a bonus by ensuring
that McNally is taught a lesson.'

'Kill him you mean?' said Arnie Semple.

Bradley Stockwell smiled and glanced at Heinrich
Feldmann. 'If either of us were to suggest that it
could possibly place us outside the law,' he said.
'However, if McNally should happen to get himself
killed either accidentally or by one of you in self-
defence, that is another matter. You men are the
experts in that particular field and we shall leave
exactly how you deal with him entirely up to you.'

'A bonus, you say,' said one of the other men.
'How much?'

'We were thinking in terms of two hundred
dollars,' said Feldmann.

'Make it five hundred,' replied the man. 'We all
know McNally is mighty handy with a gun, it won't be
that easy.'

'Five hundred seems a little excessive,' said
Stockwell. 'What do the rest of you think? I'd say two
hundred was a fair price.'

There followed a short period of muttering
between the men and once again there appeared to
be an unusual amount of agreement and the general
opinion was that they wanted at least $400. After a
little more haggling the amount was finally agreed at
$300.

'When do we start?' asked another man.

'As soon as you leave this bar, if you like,' said
Stockwell. 'We've been told that he will probably
leave the Lloyd farm – that's the first one you come
to in the pass – tomorrow morning.'

'Do you want witnesses to say we acted in self-
defence?' asked Phil Grayson.

'That is entirely a matter for you,' said Feldmann. 'You must remember though, that neither of us is asking that McNally be murdered.'

'We get the message loud an' clear,' said another of Feldmann's men. 'If anythin' goes wrong or we're arrested for murder, you won't lift a finger to help.'

'That is about the size of it,' nodded Feldmann. Once again the men formed little huddles and talked for some time. Eventually Jess Smith and Gus Tranter left the bar.

'You can count me an' Jess out of it,' said Gus as they left. 'Take a look at us, neither of us would stand a chance even against a kid with a cork gun the way we are. Don't get the idea we're runnin' scared though, we ain't, we're just bein' realistic.'

'You are probably right,' nodded Stockwell. 'OK, what about the rest of you?'

Once Jess Smith and Gus Tranter had left there were ten men. Of these, five were plainly not very keen on the idea even though they had to admit that the possibility of earning $300 almost swayed them. In the end, after a little more talking between themselves, they too left the saloon.

'That leaves five of you,' said Feldmann. 'I'm not surprised at the others leaving and you five are the ones I would have expected to take up the offer. Arnie Semple, Phil Grayson and Sam Joiner from Mr Stockwell's side and Mick Sayers and Jim Riley from mine. We wish you the best of luck, gentlemen.'

'It won't be a matter of luck,' muttered Arnie Semple. 'McNally don't know this territory like we do.'

Brogan had thought about staying on until the first herd was safely through the pass but after some care-

ful thought he decided that he was not going achieve
anything by remaining and it just might lead to his
further involvment which he was anxious to avoid. At
about the same time – just after dawn – that Peter
Lloyd, Samuel Drummond and Paul Graham left for
Grover to sign the agreement, he saddled his horse
and headed north through the valley.

The three farmers had secured the agreement of
the community – with one or two dissenting voices –
the previous evening, when all except Brogan had
attended church to give thanks for their deliverance.
It was suggested that Brogan attend but he refused
on the grounds that he had tempted fate enough for
the moment and did not want to incur the wrath of
their God, laughingly suggesting that He just might
send down a thunderbolt and destroy the church.
Most people did not seem to see the funny side of his
remark, saying that it was most unwise of him to
tempt the Lord.

When the three young farmers rode into Grover,
the first person they met was Sheriff Gorman who
expressed relief that everyone had at last seen sense
and told them that he would be at the meeting with
the lawyer as witness to the agreement along with the
town mayor. The second person they met was Old
Tom as he sat outside the Black Diamond waiting for
it to open.

'Is McNally still up there?' he asked.

'As far as we know he rode out when we left to
come here,' said Peter Lloyd.

'Then maybe one of you ought to ride back an' tell
him there's a bounty out on his head,' said the old
man. 'Three hundred dollars.'

'How do you know this?' asked Peter.

'I hear things,' Old Tom said, smiling knowingly and tapping the side of his nose with a finger.

'I believe him,' said Paul Graham. 'The trouble is we'll never catch him now. He'll be through the valley before we could get there.'

'I do not believe that we need worry too much about Brogan,' said Peter. 'He told me last night that he was expecting someone to make an attempt on his life. Apparently such things are commonplace and he did not appear too concerned, simply saying that he had to die sometime. We shall take up the matter with Mr Stockwell and Mr Feldmann though. Sheriff Gorman will be there and he will probably be very interested.'

'Don't do anything to jeopardize this agreement,' urged Paul Graham. 'I know we owe Brogan a lot, but since he seems unconcerned at the prospect of someone trying to murder him, I suggest that we, too, should not bother too much.'

'It is a question of which is more important, I agree,' sighed Peter. 'Under other circumstances my conscience would tell me to warn him, but I really do believe that he is well aware of what might happen. Very well, all we can do is offer a prayer for his safe deliverance.'

Brogan was indeed expecting trouble in one form or another and, as ever, was fully on the alert although he did not really expect anyone to be stupid enough to do anything in the valley where there was a possibility of witnesses. On his way through, he was greeted by farmers, most of whom wished him luck and thanked him. Most of the wives insisted on plying him with parcels of home cooking, all of which he accepted because he did not want to cause offence to anyone even though Mary Lloyd had ensured that he was well supplied. As he passed the church, the pastor came out to greet him and offer his thanks and Brogan was almost pleased when the pastor's wife did not give him any food.

'I was kind of surprised when you backed Peter Lloyd an' the others,' said Brogan.

'I had thought for some time that that was one of our traditions which needed to change,' smiled the pastor. 'As you no doubt have noticed, I, too, am of the younger generation. I must admit that I was surprised when it happened and also surprised when the elders so readily agreed – with a few exceptions of course. So, Mr McNally, you leave us and perhaps it is just as well. Under your influence who knows what other changes might have been suggested. We must first of all learn to walk before we start running. You are, of course, quite welcome to stay as long as you choose, perhaps even permanently.'

'Your kind of life ain't for me,' said Brogan. 'I'm a drifter an' allus will be, at least until I stop a bullet or I suddenly drop dead out in some desert. If I drop dead in the desert at least I'll still be of some use. . . .' The pastor looked questioningly. 'My body will keep a few vultures or buzzards goin' a bit longer,' he laughed.

'Quite!' grimaced the pastor. 'On the question of someone shooting you, I don't know if there is any significance or not, but my wife was unable to sleep very much and she spent quite a large part of the night out of bed. She says that at about four o'clock she saw three men riding north. She could not be certain who two of them were but she was quite definite about the other, one of Mr Stockwell's men known as Phil Grayson. She thinks one of the others was a man named Arnie Semple but she could not be certain.'

'I can't say as I'm too surprised,' said Brogan. 'OK, thanks for the warnin', I'll be on the lookout for 'em.'

It took longer for him to reach the head of the valley than he had expected, but then he had been stopped frequently, and it was a little over two hours after leaving the Lloyd farm that Brogan was riding over a crest, about 100 yards wide between the hills at the head of the valley. For a brief moment he stopped and looked back, not because he was interested or had any feeling of regret at leaving since he had never been anywhere he had regretted leaving behind, but because for the last half-hour he had had the feeling that he was being followed and it was very rare that his feelings were wrong. This occasion did not prove an exception since it did not take very long to confirm his suspicions as he saw two men on horseback and it was plain that they were not farmers since he had not seen even one horse which could be classed as a riding animal, all he had seen were mules or work horses.

'That makes five of 'em,' he said to his horse. 'Three up ahead an' two behind. I wonder if they know about each other? OK, old girl,' he said again, 'from here on in you just keep your eyes an' ears open.' His horse nodded her head and answered with a snort.

Once over the crest, the land opened up on to a flat, brown plain, liberally dotted with clumps of stunted thorn trees, some cactus and many large boulders. The trail itself was well marked and ran fairly straight across the plain. It did not take Brogan long to establish where the most likely places for ambush were, although he had the feeling that at that moment there was nobody behind any of the rocks. Nevertheless, he drew his rifle from the saddle holster and, after checking that it was loaded, laid it across his legs. He also eased his revolver slightly but did not check it since he had done that before he left.

He was about a mile across the plain when he saw the two men following him appear over the crest at the head of the valley and he saw them hastily ride down and disappear among the brown grass and rocks. He also knew that they were taking advantage of the cover to circle across the plain and head him off. However, years of experience had taught him to read all the signs, such as birds, as they suddenly flew into the air when they were disturbed and he had little difficulty in being able to tell exactly where the men were.

After some time he came across a small stream and decided that if there was going to be a showdown, it might as well be on his terms. He allowed his horse to roam free, which was quite normal, and made his preparations. . . .

'He's stopped by that creek,' said Mick Sayers. 'That looks like his horse over there. I can't see him though, maybe we'd better hang back for a while.'

'No, the sooner we take him the better. Leave the horses here,' said Jim Riley, 'You go round that way' – he indicated to the right – 'and I'll go that way. We'll trap him between us. He can't shoot in both directions at once.'

'OK,' agreed Sayers. 'We'll give each other ten minutes to get in position.'

'Don't take no chances,' advised Riley. 'As soon as you can, just blast him with everythin' you've got.'

The two men slowly circled until they were each within sight of the figure sitting alongside the creek but could not see each other. They were both still slightly out of range and had to ease their way forward. Mick Sayers reached a large rock, about six feet high, with quite a large thorn tree growing behind it. From the base of the rock he had a clear view of the creek and the man sitting alongside it and he was now well within rifle range. He licked his lips, raised the rifle and took careful aim. . . .

The only sound to escape Mick Sayers' lips was a rasping gasp; the knife slid silently across Mick's yielding throat in the same instant that Brogan leapt from the rock to straddle his victim's back and blood gushed messily on to Brogan's hands and arms. Eventually he stood up and wiped his knife and hands on Mick Sayers' jacket and glanced across the creek, but it seemed that his actions had gone unnoticed.

Slitting a man's throat was not usually a method which Brogan chose, although he had done so on one or two occasions in the past. However, it normally had the advantage of being quiet and quite quick and efficient. He had chosen the method this time simply because it was too difficult to do anything else without risking alerting the other man. He now crouched and waited for things to happen on the opposite side of the creek.

It was about a minute later when at least three shots suddenly echoed round and the figure sitting by the creek tipped forward, its head apparently in the water. Another shot followed and a voice suddenly shouted, seemingly very pleased with himself.

'Got him!' yelled Jim Riley. 'I got the bastard. What the hell happened to you, Mick? I reckon I can claim that three hundred all for myself.' The voice suddenly transformed itself into flesh as Jim Riley appeared on the bank. He kicked the body by the water and suddenly looked about in fear. 'Hell . . . Mick, where are you?'

'Lyin' right by my feet,' rasped Brogan, showing himself, his rifle at his shoulder. 'Nice try, but you should've known better. . . .' Jim Riley wildly raised his rifle but crumpled to the ground under a volley of three shots.

'Two down, three to go,' grunted Brogan with a certain amount of satisfaction.

An hour later he had strapped the bodies across their horses and had sent the animals back along the trail towards the pass on the basis that the horses were likely to head for the nearest farm.

TEN

The remainder of that day proved completely uneventful, much to Brogan's surprise. Although the land was fairly flat, there had been plenty of places where ambush was possible and he could only think that perhaps the other three men had not tried anything because they were being very careful or – but most unlikely, he thought – they had not been sent to deal with him.

That night he made camp alongside a small creek and opened up one of the many parcels of food he had been given. He had lost track as to who had given him what but the one he opened contained a large piece of fresh bread, half a roast chicken and two cold potatoes. When he had eaten this, out of little more than idle curiosity, he opened the remaining eight parcels and discovered that all but one contained the same, chicken, potatoes and bread. The one exception contained a piece of venison instead of chicken and a piece of cheese. However, he did not mind, such things counted as luxuries in his normal life. The only trouble was that he had so much that he knew he would be unable to eat it all before it started to go off.

He was in completely unknown territory and although he knew that he must be on the road to Banksville – where the railroad was – he had no idea how far it was. He was up at dawn as usual the following morning and, after eating another of his parcels of food, continued on his way at his normal leisurely pace.

At mid-morning, he approached a fairly large, circular hill, which seemed out of place in the otherwise flat landscape and he decided to climb up it and view the terrain ahead through his spyglass.

The hill proved to be an old Indian burial ground, a place no self-respecting Indian would ever be found. Most settlers he knew also tended to avoid such places, partly because of a natural fear of burial grounds in general, but mainly because they did not want to offend the local Indian tribes. However, such places held no fear for Brogan and for about half an hour he scanned the land ahead for signs of activity. He eventually decided that the way ahead was clear and returned to his horse.

He had not completely wasted his time, he had gained a good impression of just what lay ahead and had seen what appeared to be a wide river perhaps eight or nine miles away. It appeared that if he wanted to continue in the direction he was travelling he would have to cross the river. He did not particularly like the idea but it meant turning either east or west and he might very well still have to make the crossing.

The river was reached about an hour after midday and from a small rise he could see that it was about 300 yards wide and that there was apparently a ferry across. He assumed that any cattle would have to swim for it but since it did not appear fast flowing that would probably present no problem. However, he had absolutely no intention of swimming across and for some time he also had doubts about using the ferry. Eventually, and after a long conversation with his horse, he put his doubts to one side and opted to make the crossing.

There was a solitary shack alongside a small, mud ramp and at first there did not appear to be anyone there, but after a few loud calls a bleary-eyed man, about his own age, grumpily appeared, closely followed by a very fat and sheepish-looking Indian woman who was in the process of fastening her dress.

'Gettin' so's a man can't have no peace,' grumbled the man. 'This is twice in one day someone has wanted to get across. That'll be two dollars.'

'Two dollars!' grunted Brogan. 'Ain't that a mite expensive?'

'Two dollars,' the man grumbled again. 'It's two dollars for one man an' his horse an' it's two dollars for five men an' horses it takes the same time to get a boatload across as one man. You can allus swim if you've a mind to, it don't matter a toss to me.'

Brogan had to admit that there was a certain amount of logic in the man's point of view and nodded. 'OK, two dollars it is,' he agreed, and delved into his pocket to count out the required two dollars in small change. The ferryman did not even bother to count it but stuffed it into his pocket. 'You say I'm the second trip across today?' he asked. 'How long ago was the first?'

'Four hours,' muttered the man. 'Three men an' three horses.'

'I don't suppose you happened to hear what their names were?' Brogan asked.

'Mister,' grunted the man, 'I don't ask nobody who they are, where they're goin' or where they're from, information like that can be dangerous. Only thing I do know about 'em, just the same as I know about you, is that they must've come from Grover an' they is more'n like headed for Banksville, but that's 'cos there ain't nowhere else they could've come from or be goin' to.'

'Could they go to anywhere else but Banksville?'

'Maybe they could,' nodded the man. 'But it wouldn't make no sense. East brings you to Granite Canyon an' means you have to cross the river again, an' west means you have to cross the mountains, an' believe me, unless you're a mountain goat that ain't easy. Are you followin' those men?'

'I thought you didn't ask no questions?' laughed Brogan.

The man shrugged. 'I'll be ready in about half an hour,' he said. 'In the meantime, you can have the use of my shack an' my squaw for a dollar.'

'I'm right off luxuries,' grinned Brogan. 'Meanin' no disrespect, ma'am.' The woman smiled broadly and thrust out her huge chest, but it was plain that she did not really understand what Brogan was saying, but she soon got the message that he was not interested and waddled off to the shack.

'They must've said somethin',' prodded Brogan as the man prepared to launch the ferry.

'They didn't say nothin' as far as I'm concerned,' muttered the ferryman.

Brogan pulled a $5 bill from his pocket and waved it temptingly in front of the ferryman. 'This says that they did,' he said with a grin.

The man looked at the money for a moment and

licked his lips before replying. 'One of 'em was called Arnie, I heard the others call him that, an' I think one of 'em was Phil, or somethin' like that. I never heard what the third one was called.' He reached for the money but Brogan snatched it away.

'I know who they are,' he said. 'I don't pay for information I already know. Arnie Semple an' Phil Grayson, they work for a rancher named Stockwell back at Grover. You'll have to do better'n that if you want this money. I reckon they must've said somethin' about me.'

The ferryman licked his lips again but this time he seemed frightened of something. 'They didn't say nothin',' he said eventually. 'Nothin' at all. You can keep your money.'

Brogan felt a tingle run down his spince. He knew that the man was frightened enough to refuse almost any amount of money and he also knew that from that moment on he would have to have all his senses working overtime. He pocketed the note and allowed the ferryman to continue his work, work which seemed to be taking far longer than it should. Eventually, Brogan was leading his horse on to the ferry and the boat was pushed away from the bank.

Although the ferryman used a long pole to push the flat-bottomed boat along for the first few yards, there was a rope anchored to the bank which then passed between stout uprights either end of the boat and the ferryman laid down the pole and took up the rope and started to haul the boat along. In a very short time he was soaking wet as the water ran out of the rope.

'How long does it take?' asked Brogan, scanning the bank ahead for any sign of possible ambush.

Although he could not swim he was prepared to throw himself overboard if necessary and hope for the best.

'About twenty minutes,' grunted the ferryman. 'You in a hurry?'

'Nope,' admitted Brogan, 'It's just that this is too open for my likin'.'

The man grunted something but Brogan was not really listening, more concerned with what lay ahead, which appeared to be nothing. There was no sign of activity of any kind on the bank opposite.

The boat reached a large pole obviously placed in the river to guide the rope and the ferryman bent down into the water and picked up a second rope. The first rope was released from the uprights and the second slid into position. Although Brogan was aware of what was happening, he was not really taking that much notice. The first indication he had that something was very wrong came as the ferryman once again bent down, this time his back towards Brogan, and then suddenly swung round holding a shortened shotgun. The shot and the splash Brogan made as he fell into the water came in almost the same instant as Brogan reacted more or less by pure instinct. The fact that he was unable to swim was of no consideration whatsoever.

He had expected the water to be deep, but Brogan felt his feet sinking into soft mud and, still holding his breath, he looked up and could see the ferryman now standing at the edge of the boat, apparently pointing his gun at him. He lunged against something hard and found himself underneath the boat. By this time his lungs were almost bursting and he had to come up for air. He used the last of his breath and seemingly all his strength to push and claw his way under the boat to the front, where he hoped the ferryman would not be expecting him. Fortunately for him, he was right as he noisily broke the surface, took a deep breath and once again ducked beneath the boat. The noise of the ferryman's boots as he ran to the front could be plainly heard.

The water was little more than five feet deep and Brogan knew that he could stand up quite easily. However, he found what appeared to be a very firm footing and held his breath for as long as he could, watching the jiggling shapes above him and listening for the sound of the ferryman's boots.

Once again he was forced to surface for air, this time coming up at the stern, taking one quick gulp and disappearing again. Once again the sound of the ferryman running to the stern could be plainly heard. This time Brogan was ready, and again, acting purely by instinct, as he saw the indistinct shape of the ferryman apparently bend over the stern in order to see beneath the water more easily, he suddenly launched himself with all his force off the rock on which he was standing, his arms outstretched. . . .

The speed with which Brogan shot out of the water obviously caught the ferryman off guard and Brogan's hands managed to clutch the man's coat. The very force of Brogan falling back into the water dragged the man after him.

There then followed a period when even Brogan was uncertain as to whether the ferryman was fighting him or was struggling to get himself to the surface. In the end Brogan decided that the man was panicking. He managed to get hold of the man from behind, wrapped his legs firmly round the man's waist and, with both hands, forced the man's head under water. Both men struggled together for about five minutes before the ferryman's body suddenly seemed to go limp. Brogan struggled with the body to the rock, found the rope and heaved the body over it. He then somehow managed to heave himself into the boat and, after a short time during which he gasped and spluttered to catch his breath, Brogan reached down and pulled the ferryman into the boat. The man was apparently still alive and Brogan laid him on the flat bottom, face down, and waited. . . .

Exactly how long Brogan waited for the man to recover, he had no idea and did not care that much. He had heard of people having water pumped out of their lungs but since he had no idea how to perfom this feat and even less interest as to whether or not the man survived, he simply waited.

The man coughed and spluttered, wheezed and groaned, and eventually he was able to raise his head and stare, almost unseeingly at Brogan. This time Brogan sat at the side of the boat toying with his revolver just in case the man should get any strange ideas. Brogan said nothing, prepared to wait until the man was able to sit up.

'OK, mister,' grated Brogan, deliberately pointing his gun at the ferryman's head and cocking the hammer with his thumb. 'Just what was all that about?'

'I don't know what you're talkin' about.' wheezed the man.

'Don't give me that crap,' said Brogan. 'This

revolver needs tryin' out after the soakin' it's just had. Your head will be the perfect thing to try it out on.'

The ferryman studied the gun for a moment and then shrugged, a half smile appearing on his face. 'They paid me to kill you,' he grunted. 'He's just a dirty old saddlebum, they said.'

'How much did they give you?'

'Ten dollars,' he replied. 'It warn't much, I know, but I once killed a man for less'n two dollars, an' out here ten dollars is no mean sum. There ain't that much to spend it on 'ceptin' when I go into Banksville, which is about twice a year.'

'And what were you to do with my body?' asked Brogan.

'They said as they'd be back this way the day after tomorrow.' he said. 'I was to keep your body. Seems they wanted it for proof.'

'They wanted it to collect whatever bounty had been put out on me,' said Brogan. 'I can assure you that it was a whole lot more'n ten dollars.'

'Yeh, well, maybe so,' nodded the man. 'Anyhow, I was to get another ten dollars if you was dead when they came back, as well as any money I found on you an' anythin' I could get for your horse, saddle an' guns. I could've been quite rich.'

'You'd've got a bullet more'n like,' said Brogan. 'OK, you tried an' you failed, now get this boat across this river, I don't like water.'

'Ain't you gonna kill me?' gulped the man.

'I just might if'n you don't get your muscles on that rope an' get us over there,' threatened Brogan.

Ten minutes later Brogan was leading his horse off the ferry, having ascertained that the three men had

ridden off in the direction of Banksville which was
about two days away.

The ferryman may have told Brogan that Banksville
was about two days away, but he neglected to tell him
that on the way there was a tumble-down shack which
was proclaimed by a twisted sign to be a saloon and
diner. This was about an hour after leaving the ferry.

Brogan studied the shack from the safety of a
clump of trees about 400 yards from it and at first it
seemed that the place was completely empty.
However, four horses in the paddock just behind the
shack told him that someone must be about.
Eventually, after about half an hour, a solitary figure
appeared at the door of the shack for a few moments.
As far as Brogan was concerned there was no mistaking that it was Arnie Semple.

It seemed a fairly simple matter to bypass the
shack without too much risk of being seen and this
was what he elected to do. He did not ride, instead
he led his horse in a wide arc round to the left,
following a depression in the ground. However, for
one of the few times in his life, Brogan had read the
terrain incorrectly and very soon found himself
entering a bog. At first he tried to negotiate it but
after some time was forced to admit defeat and
retrace his steps. He tried an even wider arc but that
way appeared even worse and eventually he found
himself back at his starting point.

The way round to the right was just as bad and it
seemed that the only firm ground lay straight ahead
and appeared to be about 100 yards wide. He considered his position for a few moments and, after once
again consulting his horse, he decided that he had

no alternative but to carry on and face the men. He sighed, checked that his revolver had suffered no permanent damage from its soaking in the river, checked his rifle and then mounted.

'OK, old girl,' he said. 'I guess we'll just have to play this one by ear.'

However, it seemed that luck was on his side as three men suddenly appeared from the shack, saddled their horses and then rode off in the opposite direction. He smiled and waited for about ten minutes to allow them to get well away before moving on.

It seemed that the owner of the shack had seen him approach as he met him at the door, the man carrying a rifle although not actually threatening Brogan with it. Casually Brogan slid his Colt from its holster and toyed with it.

'Reckon you can get the first shot in?' he said to the owner.

'Nope,' grunted the man. 'An' I ain't about to try either. I allus carry this . . .' – he shook the rifle – 'just in case. I get some funny folk through here sometimes.'

'I know,' grinned Brogan, 'I just seen three of 'em leave.'

'You must be McNally,' said the man. 'They said you might just come through, although they did say they'd made some arrangements for you.'

'Those arrangements went wrong,' said Brogan. 'Where are they headin' now?'

'They said somethin' about goin' to Banksville,' replied the man.

'That far?' said Brogan. 'I hear it's about two days away.'

'That's what they said,' muttered the man. 'You want somethin' to eat?'

Brogan laughed. 'Nope, I'm particular about what I eat an' where.'

'Suit yourself,' grunted the man.

'I will,' assured Brogan. 'What's the lay of the land like up ahead?'

'Flat an' boggy.'

'Guessed as much,' Brogan smiled. 'OK, I guess I'll be on my way.' He urged his horse forward and nodded at the man as he passed. He had only travelled a few yards when he sensed rather than heard something and suddenly he swung round in his saddle, gun in hand.

As far as he could remember there was only one shot, the one from his gun. The man looked startled, dropped the rifle which had been at his shoulder, and slowly crumpled to the ground. The sudden twist of his body must have affected the wound on Brogan's head as he suddenly felt very giddy and everything went hazy. . . .

When he came to, Brogan found himself on the ground with his horse standing over him. A glance towards that shack showed a body Iying on the ground, apparently lifeless. After a short time he struggled to his feet, felt the bandage still around his head and decided that he had not done any more damage. He went over to the body, which even then was swarming with flies around the blood soaking through his shirt. The man was quite dead.

'I suppose they paid you ten dollars as well,' he muttered. 'You weren't quite so lucky as the ferryman.'

Whether it was the heat of the day or because of

his fall he did not know, but he felt thirsty and looked about for some water. Although there was plenty of it about, it all looked very unsavoury and he went into the dingy interior of the shack, where he found a small counter, a long, rough, wooden table with benches either side and a pot full of something that looked unmentionable and smelled even worse. He went behind the counter and found several bottles of what he assumed was home-made whiskey. There was also a jug of what looked like very cloudy beer but which in actual fact tasted quite good. He helped himself to a large glass of it.

It seemed that the man had lived alone since there was no sign of anyone else and the shack consisted of a single room with four beds at the far side, all of which looked as if the blankets had never been changed. There was a stove in the centre of the room on which a pan of water was steaming.

Glass of beer in hand, he went outside, glanced at the body, but was suddenly listening hard. There was no doubt about it, riders were coming his way. He looked again at the body, listened and then acted. . . .

Arnie Semple, Phil Grayson and Sam Joiner hitched their horses to the rail and stomped noisily into the shack, demanding to know where 'Slim', the owner was. When there was no response they helped themselves to a bottle of whiskey and slouched at the table, laughing and swearing.

'Wonder if that ferryman managed to deal with McNally,' laughed Semple. 'It sure looks like it since he ain't reached here yet.'

'We'll find out tomorrow,' said Sam Joiner. 'Then we pay the man off.'

'Yeh,' laughed Grayson. 'With a bullet!'

'Where the hell is Slim?' demanded Semple, looking about. 'Slim!' he called out. 'Where the hell are you, we want some food!'

'He's otherwise engaged!' said Brogan. The three men looked in a mixture of amazement, disbelief and horror as Brogan suddenly swung down upside down in front of them, his legs hooked over a beam in the low roof and with a revolver in each hand. Although he was not really a left-handed shot, he could use one if necessary and he had found the second revolver behind the counter. 'Howdy, gentlemen, I sure am pleased to meet you again.'

The two benches on which the men were sitting suddenly crashed to the floor as each struggled to pull his revolver. Brogan had plenty of time and it only required three shots and the three men either crashed to the floor or, in the case of Sam Joiner, almost broke the table as he fell on to it.

Brogan eased himself off the beam, looked at the three bodies and decided that they were dead. Suddenly he was listening hard again. More horses, this time coming from the same direction he had come. There was no time to hide the bodies so Brogan stood at the counter and waited. He did not have to wait long; three horses pulled up and shortly afterwards a shadowy figure appeared in the doorway, gun plainly at the ready.

'Evenin', Sheriff,' said Brogan. 'A long way off your territory, ain't you?'

'McNally!' gasped Sheriff Sam Gorman. 'Hell, you could've got yourself killed.'

'That's what they thought,' said Brogan stepping forward and nodding at the three men on the floor.

The sheriff stepped inside and was immediately followed by Peter Lloyd and Paul Graham.

'I told you we needn't have worried about him,' said Peter Lloyd. 'What happened, Brogan?'

'Nothin' much,' said Brogan, casually. 'Nothin' I couldn't deal with.'

'So I see,' muttered Sheriff Gorman. 'Hell, I'll be glad when you're a few hundred miles from my territory. I go ten years and don't have one murder or killin' for any reason an' suddenly you come along an' turn everythin' upside down.'

'Yeh,' laughed Brogan, 'I guess I do have that effect on folk.'

'Where's Slim, the feller who owns this rat hole?' asked Gorman.

'Round the back,' said Brogar. 'I had to kill him, too. You must've talked to the ferryman. Like him, this Slim feller was paid to kill me. He didn't live to collect though.'

'Well, you sure have a habit of spreading a lot of blood about,' said Paul Graham. 'We didn't know if we'd find you dead or not, although Peter seemed to think that we wouldn't.'

'An' fortunately he was right,' said Brogan. 'Is that what brought you out here, lookin' for me?'

'We found out that Stockwell and Feldmann had offered three hundred dollars to the man who killed you,' said Gorman. 'That's when I decided to come after you and these two offered to come with me.'

'We found the first two across their saddles,' said Peter. 'The only thing I must ask is was it necessary to slit the man's throat?'

'I thought so at the time,' said Brogan. 'So, it seems my life is only worth three hundred dollars.

Still, I suppose every man has his price an' I don't suppose saddletramps rate very much at any time. What happens now, Sheriff?'

'You get the hell out of here an' out of my life!' rasped the sheriff. 'I reckon I've got enough trouble with the first of those herds comin' this way tomorrow an' then I have to think about if I can charge Stockwell an' Feldmann with somethin'.'

'I think that unless Mr McNally wants to pursue the matter,' said Peter, 'we can forget what happened.'

'Since the sheriff wants me out of his hair,' laughed Brogan, 'I guess I won't be doin' anythin'.'

'I'll think about it,' said Sheriff Gorman, grudgingly. 'Now, let's get these bodies together. McNally, since it was you who did the dirty work in the first place, you can put 'em across their saddles. I ain't stayin' here tonight, I like to know the bugs I share with.'

'I don't suppose the bugs would mind,' grinned Brogan. 'OK, sheriff, I'll load 'em up for you. There's just one thing: I'm a bit short on cash. If you don't mind I'll take what money I can find either on the bodies or in here. I don't want to be accused of stealin' so if'n you say I can't, I won't.'

'Well, whatever money there is ain't goin' to be much use to any of them,' grunted the sheriff. 'OK, I don't mind.'

By the time he had strapped the bodies to their horses, and searched the shack, Brogan found that he was just over forty-four dollars better off. It was not a fortune but it would see him through a few more weeks.

Sheriff Gorman and the two farmers said farewell

and started on the return journey about two hours before sunset, Sheriff Gorman still insistent that he was not going to stay the night in the shack. Brogan, however, was not particularly bothered about the prospect of bedbugs and spent the night on the cleanest looking of the beds. The following morning he put three bottles of the home-made whiskey into his bags and rode on, hoping to find a way round the town of Banksville.